LAKE
& *Other Stories*

OTHER BOOKS BY GERRY SHIKATANI

Aqueduct
1988— Selected Poems & Texts, 1973-1988
The Book of Tree: A Cottage Journal
A Sparrow's Food

LAKE

& *Other Stories*

Gerry Shikatani

THE MERCURY PRESS

The publisher gratefully acknowledges the financial assistance of the Canada Council and the Ontario Arts Council, as well as that of the Government of Canada through the Multiculturalism Directorate of the Department of Heritage.

Cover design by TASK
Edited by Beverley Daurio
Cover art by
Composition and page design by TASK

Printed and bound in Canada by Metropole Litho
Printed on acid-free paper
First Edition
1 2 3 4 5   00 99 98 97 96

Canadian Cataloguing in Publication Data

Shikatani, Gerry
    Lake & other stories
ISBN 1-55128-039-6
I. Title. II. Title: Lake and other stories.
PS8575.H47L35 1996   C813'.54   C96-931715-8
PR9199.3.S55L35 1996

Represented in Canada by the Literary Press Group
Distributed in Canada by General Distribution Services

The Mercury Press
137 Birmingham Street
Stratford, Ontario
Canada   N5A 2T1

On Actions

The solitary process of these acts of writing was nevertheless nurtured in innumerable ways by community.

I am grateful to Richard Truhlar, Steven Ross Smith and Brian Dedora who for several years organized the Kontakte Writers-in-Performance series in Toronto. It attracted a community of artists which included Owen Sound and The Horsemen who gave me support and space to create, learn and exchange. The Link Poetry Workshop and Ted Plantos and Hans Jewinski first provided me a place for my work.

My sincerest gratitude to the following people for taking the time to read or listen to some of these stories and offering invaluable suggestions: Jan Conn, Mary di Michele, Wayne Keon, Mitsuko Shikatani, Lola Lemire Tostevin, June Shiozaki, Daniel David Moses and Steven Ross Smith.

I am especially indebted to writers sean o'huigin and the late sha(u)nt basmajian for their remarkable generosity.

These stories are for them, my siblings, and Iris Watts Shikatani, Ron Onami, George Shiozaki, Roy Horikawa, Franziska Lange and their families, who have shown me how family grows beyond, to a larger world.

I am further grateful to The Canada Council, the Ontario Arts Council and those publishers who supported me through the Writers' Reserve Programme for the generous financial assistance which enabled me to complete this work.

Above all, I thank my editor Beverley Daurio for supporting my fiction attempts over the years, and bringing her creative eye to these stories.

ABOUT AIKO SUZUKI

Over the years since the internment of Japanese Canadians during World War II, Aiko Suzuki has been one of a handful of Japanese-Canadian artists who have, for younger Nikkei, remained models of the excellence which follows uncompromising invention, dedication, and artistic integrity.

— *Gerry Shikatani*

Contents

Lake

And there is the sound of metal, the lid of a green tackle box, with its lures, hooks and small lead weights, its filament test-line, snapping shut. A threatening hook which is caught, hanging over-rim outside, a jam to closure. It could, this barb, catch on a fall sweater, a rust-coloured pullover. It is early October, the weekend before Thanksgiving, the weekend of fall foliage tours, leaves of scarlet, yellow and rust, good weather for fishing, last of the season.

They sit facing each other at rest, propped upon each other's quiet, as he rows the aluminum skiff, outwards, with the instinctive steadying keel of push and pull. This, even though he is now over seventy, this effortless focus of intelligent strength built through his past, those days in his twenties, a fisherman in northern BC, when he'd manoeuvre his sailboat, the sailboat first, before he had finally saved enough to purchase the Kana I, gasboat through the high seas beyond Skeena River.

'I wish I could have returned sooner, father,' she says. She wonders whether she should ask... 'Mother. Did mother say much?' She wants to somehow ask this, about those few days before, in the hospital, and how he felt that first night after. And at this point, her eyes focus on his moving hands as they pull at the oars, she cannot help picturing him sitting at the kitchen table, back pencil-straight against the gray-green vinyl and chrome chair. But they do not ask such personal questions. After all, it is family.

She lies back, elbows resting on the sides of the boat. Above her the sky is a blue almost white to her eyes. 'Every now and then... every now and then, father, I think about it. How it must have looked in there, with all those machines.' She does not look at him as he rows, feeling the constancy of movement, his strength, thinks about how he never once talked about those days, that first day after, walking through the front door past the porch, the forsythia bush. But they do not ask such personal questions, after all, it is family.

'You know, if I'd come back just a bit sooner, for Easter — ('Hello... Hello... Hello... What'reya having, mother? Ham?' A voice trailing, then brittle, snapping back, coiled metal wire, the late afternoon light against the glass door of the telephone booth. 'Who's over? Kevin?' The stiff metal coiled telephone wire, the musical notes answering the sequence of buttons, numbers skipping long-distance, and then 'Hello... Hello... Oh.') — All those machines.'

He pulls hard and evenly, the boat feels like nothing beneath her, he nods once at her words, it is all, the sky clear above them, the deep lake, it is clear too, opening beyond and behind.

It was Easter that year. An Easter which will remain with her now, a phone booth on a quiet Paris street, it was not far from the Pantheon. 'But I thought — I was there at the ticket agent, I was...' her voice wandering, 'And so, when they told me I had to book twenty-one days in advance for..........It seemed okay. God, you know...' She dips her left hand to trail in the water as the skiff keeps pushing, her hand a resistance which cuts a V-stream, spreading into the green-black mirror which is lucent and steady where there can be no probe, no penetration of clear light.

He is silent at the stern. He looks up to the rocky point of pinkish and gray granite, sun angling off irregular points, the driftwood which in the lake looks like antlers, like bones sculptured with twisted wire in the shallows, the fireweed, too, stiff in the filtered light, the bones, skeletal, which look, as they drift closer, like driftwood, only driftwood...

She points a finger, without speaking. Half-way up the steep perpendicular rockface, likely a tamarack or spruce nestled on a jut, like a bird, and also a perched gray bird, or is it a rock, gray... And still closer, the twisted wire in the shallows, the fireweed too, stiff in the filtered light, the bones, skeletal, which look, as they drift closer, like driftwood, only driftwood, the place bad for snags.

(And just above, above her notice, like a figure standing, is a tree. It is a young tree, but already, in its place, it has that sense of the inevitable, the natural world, that here is the one place for its solitary stand, to grow here and here only.)

She sits silently for some time, watches him, her father. He sits on the gray tweed chair with its pink wool crochet throw, he is looking through the screened porch to the moon-twinned lake. Two white discs, as sensuous as glass marbles, the best ones clinking barely in a soft purple cloth bag, in which came the thick bottle of Crown Royal whiskey. He thinks of when he first saw her, his wife Hana, when they were coming out of Strathcona Public School in Powell River, the school upon the hillside overlooking the harbour, this year it would be forty-nine years past. Almost fifty.

'Almost fifty years, Sue... you know, ya, when you think of it,' he says, thinking out loud. And behind them, the breeze as it snaps shut a screen door of another cottage, perhaps fifty metres away, two youngish couples from near Peterborough, it is a gentle wind this thrush-thrush through the poplars, the white birches, the feathery white pines. 'Winds light tonight..... down to a low of eight.....' trails through the ear from a radio, while through the woods carries the thrush-thrush, thrush-thrush, twigs and leaves falling, blowing onto the bracken paths.

Across Sue's face he catches a draught of striped moonlight; a fish dives with its comet of colour, a millisecond wire of suspense. Splash. A dark silver coin surfaces in a pool.

There is silence, possibly lasting a few seconds, perhaps many minutes. Splash.

She looks at her tanned legs, rides the fingers of her right hand across her right leg, the long black hairs.

'Why do you leave that? The hair isn't like a woman.' he tells her firmly. 'Ask your aunt — about her... and your mother too.'

She stares at him seriously, but it is brief. This is not anger or impatience. Her mouth drops open very slightly, takes in air. When she tastes, she tastes her tongue, the water.

While they sit, the coffee is being boiled by Kevin on the wood stove. There are eggshells in the coffee, to settle the grains to the bottom of the aluminum saucepan. He adds a bit of salt, as his father does to the percolator basket at home. Underfoot, his rubber-soled runners, tracked-in sand to be swept from the gray-painted pine floor, sand left everywhere in each of the rooms which are separated by presswood partitions. They have bought local homebaked white bread from the tuckshop which they will cut into thick slices for 'before-bed' coffee, spread it with the IGA Mrs. Lee's Strawberry Jam.

She is thinking about her mother now, how she died. He is thinking about her mother too, the garden back in downtown Toronto, the forsythia bush, brilliant yellow in May, having coffee on the front porch on Sunday evenings, his only day off, when Mary, Hana's widowed sister, would drop by, and Hana and she would always end up laughing and laughing. And inside, the electric fan would be turning left-right-to-left, the current of air; and through the sound of the breeze, those 'light winds,' the moon-twinned lake. One moon in the lake of the dark night sky, one other equally brilliant in the clear night lake.

For a long time he is silent. 'You okay, father?'

'Yes.'

Again he becomes silent, it is extended.

It is like his anger — long, cool. She stares at him seriously, but it is brief. She breathes out. She is looking straight ahead, but glimpses her father's soft look upon her shoulders. His anger is long, has always felt extended, yet without drama. And yet his voice, not loud but sharp, has always registered command, immediate attention, the point of obedience.

'Do we have enough can cream, Sue?' he asks, just at the point she too has asked this to herself, the smell of a breeze, the smell of saucepan coffee filling her mouth.

When they, she and Kevin, were kids, he would flick on the light switch in the early morning, still dark outside behind the cream-coloured blind of her window. 'Wake up! You'll be late for school.' It really was a bark, this command, would make both Kevin and her feel an instant burning in the stomach, the tips of their ears, no questions to be tried. Was too, she thought, even like times that flash in reprimand when she, her stomach full of confusion and hurt, wanted to shout rebellion, and somehow he was right, was no question or reason. But here, she listened to the tick of his breathing, this silent time she wanted to hold on to like the dark sky, as he held close to his lips the pale blue mug of coffee. He drank.

'Ahhh. Good.'

She likes the feel of flannelette, its brush on skin, so that when the weather turns warm, she resists to the end the shift to a lighter summer nightgown. And later, with the shortening days of September, the approach of autumn with its cool nights, she thinks of the soft again of washed flannelette, as much as others speak of waking to cold sheets on a brisk sunny morning, the weight of two thick blankets pressing the body in bed.

And it was this way then, back then, too. Felt always like this, the soothing worn cloth, the ragged tired look, each time more, each time she pulled it from the pile of neatly folded sheets and towels when it came back from the laundry in those tall bags of thick brown paper. Snow White, Old Weston Road, Toronto. Snow White, it said.

Such nights those were when she could pull the nightgown over her head, take the flashlight and read her magazines which her mother had brought back from the houses she cleaned. She could hardly wait. Hollywood and Movie Mirror. Mrs. Cunningham was very nice, her mother had so often said. And there was, especially, True Confessions. 'Mrs. F. Cunningham,' the address label read on those magazines. And soon, after twice nodding momentarily off, she'd draw back the red-button switch of the flashlight, as into her sheets, drop off to sleep.

When her head leaves the pillow, there is a spot of blood there, dark, small, it has now almost dried, left on flat fitted sheets. The room is brilliant, almost white, and at her eyes, Sue feels the sharp grit of night, the morning tears, the pull of dry skin stretched at her eyelids and forehead, hair falling across, grazing, tickling. As her head leaves the pillow, there is a spot left there, now a brick-red coin on the pale blue percale, brushed each day, and the breeze clears the room, a room almost white and left behind.

'Do you think there's going to be a war? she once asked him, her father as they sat for dinner in their kitchen. It was the anxious days of the Cuban Missile Crisis, days which now she only faintly recollects by the sounds her mouth makes with 'JFK' or 'Khruschev,' an image of the almost bald white-haired Soviet hammering a UN desk with his shoe, the black and white aerial shots, the blurred blow-up of a precise-dot image which had been on the front page of the newspaper which her father had been reading, his click-click 'tsk' sound, tongue between teeth, near five o'clock in the afternoon, the thin smell of sliced cucumbers, the hot steam of rice, and the rich oily smell of frying fish trailing down the long hallway of their house, suspended in the sunstream from the bevelled glass window of the door.

And he answered, his voice starting up quite high in pitch, for he'd sucked in air, 'Yes,' and then lower, deeper, more concerned yet resigned, 'yes, unfortunately. It's never in our hands,' he'd said with seemingly almost no reflection. He glanced briefly downwards, before again holding with his chopsticks a piece of the crumb-fried sole which they were eating with soya sauce, wedges of lemon.

All she could do at that point was swallow a mouthful of cool dark boiled spinach, the immediacy of the ground toasted sesame, black and golden, which her mother had sprinkled over it, stuff down the warm white rice. But her eyes, round and dark, were dry with sadness and fear, the well of tears still resolved behind them.

'Why am I not crying? Kevin is. What the hell. Kevin is.' She looks over to her father, but he has gone. The aluminum skiff is empty, drifting on the deep green lake. From the shine of the pink and gray granite, from atop, where a white pine is cracked and near falling, there is a voice. As she untangles the hook from her pullover, a Northern Pike circles what looks like a lovely, smooth swimming gleam, a thin crescent.

'Kevin is, Kevin's crying.' And a crow suddenly takes flight.

'I have always been in the mountains, have always been in this mist. I am trembling as that voice which floats in ink, the depths of a wide river.' It is the voice of her father which comes clearly, and yet hangs there as in the low hovering mists. The bus winds and then moves up and out of the turn along the highway in the valley.

'The deep cuts into mudflat, wet grass and rock, it is always that one point which is the turning from the large island which marks the river's mouth. Here we together float from word to word and the gigantesque of rocks and fallen fir in the cold tidal current, turn from that large island towards the sandbars and pilings, the board-walk waving me home. It is there we have always heard the calls from Finntown, from the Tsimshian netters, too, their smell of animal, smoke and oolichan oil.'

She presses her face closer to the window, as the bus continues further along the Skeena River, where her father once fished on the north coast. And she is attracted by the trail of birds moving together like a cloud from one tree to another, at a distant point on the far side of the water, mountains even beyond.

Behind the glass, she can only guess at the damp air and the wind. And yet under her thick autumn clothing and within her chest, she feels what she imagines is the pace of the sky's current flashing past her, and in this the undulating timbres of his voice.

'I have been dreaming,' says her father, it is the break so blue in the storm clouds where I take his burning cedar, the dry twigs of the salmonberry the scent of that foliage pushed to my face. He speaks again:

'Sometimes so obscured by the foliage of the wood found behind our house, seated in the mountain, which marks the bend in this endless river.'

And for just one brief moment, she catches a glimpse of the eagle over the Skeena, where water meets water, the Ecstall River's current. The eagle sits dead-still within the clouds which snake as frequent rain, the weights which are wind-carried, attendant in the black mountains.

'And whose voice back of this place,' Father asks, his voice deep in my head, 'our cracking fires which we stoke, and the blooms of wild huckleberry, the great pine mushrooms in the damp soil? The one the one who comes with the Finntown, comes with Tsimshian too, a ghost-voice, "Darling" I want to name, I want this name too much for myself.'

'Look, it's time, isn't it time you put on your shortie?' her mother had always teased. It was thin smooth cotton, sleeveless and pale blue — baby blue — ribbed with white lace at the armholes and neck, was summer, hot stuffy nights, the electric fan turning, returning, with its blast of cooler whirling air across the sweaty backs of her knees as she felt the gradual slowing of her breaths.

'You need a new one. We'll pick up a new flannelette one at Eaton's, what do you think?' her mother would say in the first days of September. But even then, though the brushed cotton had become so threadbare that it had ripped at the hips and right shoulder when she'd once twisted not extraordinarily one night, she still loved the weary pilled cloth and its small pink flowers gone faint, almost disappearing. And she would push face first into the pillow, burying herself, brush her wrists and forearms against the glorious air-chilled fabric of pillowcase, her legs sweeping in butterfly movements under the weight which became nothing, falling off, became eventually the morning, the butterfly movements again, the exquisite October, full of brittle light.

And it has always been true, continued like this on and on since her teens, the feeling beneath the loose fabric. And she rubs her hand to her right cheekbone, the smell of a fine rose cream lotion, smell from the open jar on the bureau, warm beneath the lamp, giving off a shimmering pink light through its shade, the feel of an astringent on the skin, pulls a bobby pin from her hair, holds it in her teeth. Motion, a circling motion of her palm, to the abdomen, rising to her chest, to her arms. Over her head of long black hair she pulls on the nightgown, letting it tumble across her belly, the delicate hairs, the abdomen with its wrinkled brown appendectomy scar, falls about her, the comforting flannelette, the slight tick of its curled store label at the neck. She is sweeping her feet in butterfly action; and two hours later, still awake, opens her eyes to the sharp aqua digital numbers in the darkness, 1:31 a.m., and still asking the body to not focus, calming the muscles, the breaths, and her eyes twitch beneath the wiped skin of her closed lids.

How she felt, she, the loved one, the object of one dying, slipping from her hands. Holding the flesh now breathing more easily, more regularly, though in short breaths, yet the affection, the remarkable passion of the darkness he was descending to, sending this love outwards to her. This, the laying on of hands? How she remembered him in this way, the stiff blue hospital sheets pulled up around him and how at once also, a laugh felt in her throat as she saw him more handsome than such memory as he was holding onto his nurse, his thin pale feet sliding in those white terry slippers as he moved slowly and out of breath down the hall.

It was at a dinner one time, a reception of a wedding for a cousin from Whitby just outside Toronto. He was like usual, at the hand mike, singing for the guests, in his turn. At the Red Dragon Chop Suey House, all the tables pushed together in long lines and the great platters came steaming one after another, the white-jacketed Chinese waiters, short men in slicked-back black hair, making little jokes with equal suave as waiters in hotel restaurants. Bowls of egg-drop soup with emerald green peas, shiny chunks of meat and greens with thick red sauce, noodles, noodles and yes, steamed fish with slivers of green onion, glistening with hot oil.

She had hardly been able keep from laughing when she'd looked at Kevin, her father's arms swaying as he went through the tune. Kevin wasn't looking up, he didn't have to, because he knew she knew he was uncomfortable too, his stomach rolling on the floor. Oh, that high droning pitch, some beer or folk song their father had probably learned growing up, had sung likely in the bars after docking the boat at Prince Rupert.

It was then she'd overheard someone, a woman, say, 'He's still fine-looking, but I think he must already be fifty-five or so... must be... I remember his mother in Nanaimo when we went there to the pulp mill. Is she still alive?'

And that was the way it had happened that Saturday over fifteen years ago. She had darted into the washroom, the sickly green paint, the smell of that green liquid soap, a kind of chemical air, the spring door, and darting in just in time she could barely hold in her crazy laughter. But too, the comment, only simple and complimentary, it stuck, 'He's still fine-looking... must be fifty-five or so...' something like that. Her father — this fine-looking hilarious crooner of off-key Japanese songs.

Then when the illness had caught up to him, one day he'd looked in the mirror in the parlour, didn't say a thing, but Sue saw it all in the fresh June air filled with the spice-floral scent of immaculate washing and grooming, there was the look, possibly a sigh so quiet which had somehow planted into her the sense of that time... five years ago by now...

Thinks of him always so thin and vascular and not just then, but always. And that she is too, always has been. In the summer, in mid-July near her birthday on the sixth, she'd always notice her veins would stick out prominently, make her look old, and on her arms, her legs, sometimes didn't want to wear shorts, sleeveless blouses, no, only the billowy ones of woven cotton Made in India, cool because they were woven for the steamy sub-continent. There, like here in the city, she would be vascular in the hot sunshine, would be thin, sharp.

And the water is running down the drain, being sucked in as the air is reaching out, and she scans herself in the mirror and hums a tune, at first from the radio and becomes at some bridge a playful mockery of the whiney Asian pitch of her father's bar-song. And she opens her lips, forcing up the ends, while holding the teeth to see them not quite meet with their overbite, the two ridges above her lips. She stares at the reflection and now it is the summer on the northern Ontario lake and it is ready and coming, the smell of sad coffee which has boiled with its eggshells, as a cloud robes the moon.

Perhaps it was when she was about five. Hot July, in a flat over the wide street, above the Italian florist where the smells rose up from the back kitchen one floor below. Julietta, she was foreign, and always tomatoes it seemed, and heavy oil smells, the things they did to rice she'd overheard her brother saying to their mother, wet, soggy, mixed with tomatoes, and she thought about it too much and it made her nearly nauseous in the muggy flat, the nights cockroaches would scramble behind the wall clock, the stove, when the kitchen lights were flicked on. And Julietta's voice rose up from one floor below, the sultry soprano pitch of opera, which made the brother and sister laugh and laugh, until it became aggravation.

What age was she then? And what is it she remembers from even before? Felt herself pushed, so against her mother's fresh thin body and tasted her brown-pink flesh, felt bone against bone with her jaw, as her mouth rested with familiarity around the fleshy limp nipples. Locked into the peace, the quiet dream, there was the sound of television from the living room, thin blue light beneath the door, August, humid, indeterminate time ago, canned laughter, the whine of a garbage truck, the volume faintly in her ears.

Because she had wanted so much to be there when she died — even though her mother had not been, Kevin had said, aware of anyone's presence. But then, and everyone solemnly agreed, 'You just knew she knew the family was around her,' Kevin had said, and over the months, those words of her sibling became the single image and version of her mother's death that kept forming on her lips when she lay there, trying to fall asleep, the mind flickering in the sharp helix of her bedside clock's aqua glow, 1:31; 2:31; 3:31.....

'I knew. I know you knew I was on the way,' she wrote in her journal, a kind of open letter. She typed it too, fiercely, three times, that page under her bed in the dust. And the screen door behind her is whacking shut, and it is the cool air around her, warmed by the nutty sweet scent from the kitchen.

'Coffee ready yet, Kev?' she now hears her father's voice. Shortly afterwards follows the noise of flushing from primitive plumbing. The sound of the fridge door, its tight padded weight, clicking shut.

The soft of the flannelette in the river. Fingers fall without effort into the brown foaming current of a spring. Fingers fall into the season of salmon spanwing, there are thousands — and further into the Bulkley River, the red spring, the white spring salmon, bellies white, heavy, so driven by their own nature, to be gaffed by the Tsimshian sons from Hazelton who wait suspended on ropes above the threatening water. And snow continues to fall over the towers of mountains, a fine mist and darkness in the Bulkley Valley. The map is unfolded year after year, and too cold she dips her fingers in, the soft flannelette wet to skin, but it is cold, it is the river, low throb, high-pitched voices, all, the hesitations before the dive, swimming into the heart's chamber.

Into the running current and into this, into the spawning current with leaping silver salmon — humpback and steelhead now, her face thrown back and upward to the sky and speckled with sadness and stars, the throat is moon-dry and mirror, she swallows again. Her eyes burn gently with the single moment, this, in the darkness. A voice is again calling from Finntown, the stiff wind, from the Tsimshian singer, the stiff wind, lucky dog and woodcarver of the Skeena, a low repeat like breathing which signals the smoking with alder, the catch of humpback salmon.

And again through the glass the eagle comes into her view, though barely. She thinks of walking through the tangled dry twigs and the salmonberry bushes she sees along the riverbank.

'I have always been here, always,' Sue laughs to herself, while shaking her head with a lie. 'In the mountains.' The faces, the round black eyes of her parents and brother hang about her head, long black hair, glint, of her brushing, combing out.

In the mountains, snow-capped this November, the black islands past Haysport Station on the Skeena. Mud flats, yellow grass slicked down sodden, a crab beneath rock, a bubble pops lightly in the pool, its delicate home. It is there, that point, lookout from the rails, over the depths of the river. It is always that one point which is the turning from the large island that is marker of the river's mouth. The mist in the mountains sheaths like voile the snow peaks of this month. A deer listening in the night for the hunter, aware that the echo of its own hunger is its voice in the valley, mist in the wild search of the wind. She laughs again, she laughs and laughs. She turns from the island like a compass pointer, at the mouth of this named river where her father's life is still beginning, wind filling sail, one steady captured movement through the fog.

She is in the folds of flesh, the clinging gown of her mother, taste of rose-scented water, the aureole, soft, yet it is faded. At this point, she is wordless, mouth and mother's nipple. The point which fixed, and it is the perspective of stop. Rosewater fills the eyes even shut tightly in the August bed with her, the point fixed when she smells, like a circle, smells the light wind, her mother's life, still.

It is thus in this river called Skeena; it is thus upon the river, past the deserted pilings where once the family lived, house upon stilts, the docks and net-loft only damp bones of ruin, where behind the soiled windows of the bunkhouse with its sagging green roof is an empty whiskey bottle, glass ashtray on a counter, oilrag and abandoned cigarettes. There is not a fisherman and his wife, nor a fisherman and his children, young ones who would wait for the strong knees of their father, they might rock steady on the heavy grey wool of his leg, and the current of a wide running river would be smooth as their little bodies grew weighty with sleep.

This is what is there through the soiled bus windows, or after the finger wipes away the cold blurry fog of the glass as she travels past these deserted place names of a river. The thick floating mist weaves through the black islands here and she is motionless. Sometimes does not know if memory is intact, corners with perspective. The present is damp, cold and onto the yellow rubber rainsuit she wears, jams into the face. And the river is not now memory, she thinks, and I am now in this wet weather where memory is not mist, the present I am in, floating derelict to a dock, a door to a house.

'The boat is approaching through thick mist and through the smoke of the cigarette I puff, hold at the right corner of my lips.' This is a story she recalls, told to her one summer evening by her father. He'd just begun telling it after a crazy joke she'd made as they played cards in the kitchen. A story that is now all her own.

'The boat, does it not want to see me, pays no attention but to its own route's unswerving determination?' She becomes this one evening with her father — the cards, the laughter, the strong black tea and him with his beer.

'I know I've drunk too much before supper and after, the rye on my breath, but I am cold and damp on the wheel in hand, I am in this current where somewhere I will find the float at home, boat already heavy-burden with dogfish, the oil I can sell. So I blow and blow, blow loudly my horn as warning, the terror rising from cold rubber gear gripping at my hips. 'Skipper, skipper!' I yell to no one in particular but this frightening collision in this fog. But the terrible white hull is yet relentless as it forms itself against the ground of black water. I blow, blow and before I can become truly afraid for my own life, the path of my gasboat, I am once again alone in this, only this face of mine, the rye on my breath.'

Behind the glass as she travels, she can only guess at the damp air and the wind, the story blowing into her eyes, into her throat. But through her yellow rainsuit, a damp is deep in the bones and there is the feel of the gray cloth of the bus seat rough to her neck and open hand.

Her right palm moves across the bristled fabric, against the stiff short weave. And here is the smell of transit, of express and diesel, of passing over the rises and falls of the land the shifting white centre line of the road, where mists hang over the Skeena and Ecstall Rivers. Her memory carried along on the old sternwheelers which once steamed downriver, Hazelton to Rupert, she feels this, her father's light breaths as he lies there beneath the stiff blue sheets, the rising and falling beneath the light weight of her own palm.

'I try to find the boat which is his, travelling towards our home along the river where a net-loft remains, there are yet houses left to ruin.' She watches a gasboat, its tall metal poles and wires gliding surely beneath a sky where in the distance black clouds are probably rain. And now it is her hand, fingers justly bent, fingernails gently against the upholstery, scent of faint mint and diesel in dry travelling air.

And it is not memory which is dying, for it is her father there, lying on a mattress on the tiny cabin's floor. It is spilled with the blood-whiff of fish, the knots of wet saline twine. He is in his thirties, alone in the black river night off Dehorsey Island. Her heart is reaching outwards, the words come to her insistent with desire:

'I watch the eagles and seagulls flying across the thick coniferous cedars, the wild deciduous alders, where the mountains come down to the river, tides in and out with the sea. I want to go there, pull out between all these boats, my body calm and held there in the float of steady keel. Through all these fishermen and their moored boats, to pull out alone, the gasboat, that gasboat, pulling in my nets. And then, I am squeezed into the tiny cabin, the mattress on the floor.

It is the river and the way it is, its permanence, a memory present in the current which is fading, the terror of the white-hulled ghostboat felt in the bones of her hips.

Her mind is clear, fixed stop-point on the aureole, the taste sweet and floral. She watches stilly through this window which has been streaked by the passes of night rain. There is now rosy-pink light as dawn shimmers onto the deserted pilings.

When I enter, approach mother from the kitchen, its 100-watt glare, she is looking ahead to me, but beyond yet to the wall. And she's sitting there as I've seen her times enough before, knitting, which she's let fall unattended onto her lap. Upon the wall where she is looking is the black and red-ink brush painting of a boat — a sailboat. And there is a house and a mountain floating in the distance.

'Kevin. Kevin,' my mother addresses me softly. 'Come over here to my side. I don't like the way you're coughing so much. Your health is always most important. Right?' My hand wants to touch her hair, the shiny gray strands brushed back tightly on her small head, pulled back and held neatly by two metal pins. My hand, instead, lightly falls on her shoulder. Briefly.

I do not answer, but grin slightly, look away quickly, before I ask, 'What part are you on with your knitting?' I look down at her lap, the lovely dark and light blues, greens of the yarn. 'You finished the big island part?'

And she looks at me, comforts, 'Kevin, dropping little tears? It's all right. Nothing to worry about, nothing big, they, doctor told me. You know, his family, they have always known ours.'

But I can only think the worst, what else can I do. I cannot bear the thought of loss, as I look at her smooth, though wrinkled hands, small delicate hands, which are upon the knitting on her lap, left hand resting lightly on the right. And in one corner leaning upon a small black sidetable, homemade, a neighbour gave to us before it went to the garbage, my guitar, my very pale-toned and shiny guitar is leaning.

When I was still in the last couple of years of high school, I'd found what a guitar, my music could give me. Between the notes of homework, the longing to be out on a Friday evening with a girl, or a group of friends out shooting pool, I turned the pages of songbooks, Beatles tunes mainly, some others... heard the voices of younger kids, playing outside on the street.

'Why don't you play some music?' she used to say.

'Nothing big,' I can still hear it, in my own mouth, the tightening of my throat. No tears now. I am her son.

There is no music. And I think about how she often tells me how she once played flute, wanted to become a concert flautist, but then, was enough that she had to go to work after school, cook for her father. And there is a silence.

And there is the sound of television from the next room, out of a darkness in our home. The music seems so loud.

'Kevin.'

When she looks up, Kevin is staring at his mother, has just come into the parlour. Looking at her, in the chair, behind her, he can see the rust-brown stove in the kitchen, the bright light, hear the constant hum of the fridge. Around her, balls of wool, brown, black, gray — and she is staring up at the picture on the wall over the sideboard cluttered with magazines and opened mail. She is looking peacefully at the image of the sailboat.

This is my problem, for I cannot solve what happens here, this moment when their eyes meet — or perhaps about five seconds later when he has approached her and with some hesitation, he touches her on her left shoulder, she takes his hand, places it palm open to her cheek.

I've made the coffee in the pot like this, with the eggshells, almost every night since I've been here. It's been almost seven months now. I've outlasted the last hunter of the fall, and I can hardly wait for the first snow, for the peace it brings to me. This is what I think, I guess. I have to burn the propane heater every day, morning to night. I wish it was a wood stove.

Each morning I wake up to a clock radio, one my older brother gave me a couple of years ago — a digital type with the bright aqua glow — and while I listen to the weather conditions, I sit on my bed, the rumpled mess of the flannelette sheets, the soft pilled cloth, the owners have left with me. Navy cotton shirt, sweatshirt over that, or turtleneck. How such small daily choice is always there, the beginning of day, as I look next to the time on the clock by the bed.

It only takes about a quarter of an hour in total — that I'm next down on the cool wet sand, pushing off, digging the wooden oar into the shore, then settle into the skiff, manoeuvring the oars back into their aluminum slots, the 'ki-thunk, ki-thunk' solid, assured, and I am then afloat, already the cottage shrinking in size, veiled in the mist pushing off the lake.

The highway shines, night moisture and this rain which has come with the dawn, and the bus is pulling out from the garage stop, another sleeping town, two or three fluorescent lights disappearing through the window.

She unfolds her glasses, puts them on, the sleep is still there caught in the momentary blur of her sight, the jerky movement of the bus under her, accelerating. This is the way she must travel, on this particular voyage. And now this is the way she must watch through the windows of this bus, the rain making its angular streaks across the smoked glass, the efficient motor hum of this instant. To touch the glass, the smoky haze, cold and fresh as she sits here, rose scarf wrapped softly about her neck. It is almost freezing outside, her head, an ear now pressed to the cold, the motor's hum, this instant the past is the eclipse, the thought which trails into rain.

She travels in this veiled atmosphere, a slowly moving fabric which mutes the deep morning colours — the gray of Skeena waters, the dense black-green of the forests, the giant mountains crowned with first autumn snow which blow in air woven with icy mist. It is not just that glass divides her watch from the passing geography, but that outside the water suspended in air, slowly moving, shrouding the deserted pilings, the railway markers and signs, and the sandy stretches which appear from time to time, that the fishing boats with their gillnets and seine nets of every year of the salmon run are momentarily lost in this voile, fuelled nevertheless, like fossils, by the unseen sun.

She feels it directly down there, past where she tastes the dead still air of the bus moving, and now so defined beneath the rose scarf, knotted there, a little further down yet, beneath her rust pullover, the itch beneath her chest, a light, sleepy wheeze, the light is one, luminous, bright.

It's the mist I love, cool, mysterious as I softly row out from the shore below the cottage. It takes me about ten minutes, weaving out, though I try to keep a steady line, steer my progress with balance, a true and certain cadence. I've often hoped I'd see moose — I'm told they often drink by the narrows, walled by huge rocks where also the fishing is good at dusk, some two-hundred metres — the left, to my left from the distant bed left behind. I caught one fish there once, a decent-sized smallmouth, but have never ever seen a moose. And as I steer, push and pull outward, trying to perfect my movement as I would writing a letter in my own hand, I must decide — to the left — or maybe right — where a face of pinkish and gray rock will appear as the mist thins into daylight, and I could easily see the driftwood which is there.

I am sitting on my bed, the bright aqua glow of my clock radio, the weather forecasts for the day, buzzing its trail into my head. I look up at my navy blue shirt, sweatshirt, draped over the back of a red wooden chair, the dark morning air chilling my ribs, my bony back. Or, is it that I float in this skiff, pushing and pulling, trying to perfect the movement of oars, as I would of the letters which propel the writing I feel beating in my wrist? To the left, to the right as I scan over this cold autumn lake? The orange leaves begin to gain light, the black pines jutting in a low mass upon the rocks begin to turn a shimmering blue-green.

I must decide. And I float in this skiff, the smell of dew worms, hooked fish, the smell of my father, the brief one-week summer vacations he'd yearly waited for, cherished; and I see his gray turtleneck, the one I gave him one Christmas, and he wore it afterwards so often, he'd worn only cardigans until then.

'Ah, The Brogue Shop,' he'd said, both charmed and impressed, as soon as the torn wrapping had uncovered the box it had come in.

Later, when visibility has cleared, I am steering for shore, the cottage half-way up the hill, surrounded by poplars, birch and pines, and truly it feels at last like home, though it's only a place I rent, have been there nearly seven months, since April.

I'll make some coffee, put on some toast — butter, peanut butter, jam. And it is now the words which I once again feel are a forest, from wrist to fingers, their between. And here, at such points as where the steady line of white and jack pine sometimes gives way to rockface and areas of driftwood, I am at the hazy cleft, open points of entry.

She looks at him. His face, its narrow, bony features, rounded out by the porch light, its myriad small flying insects. There is the sound of tree branches swaying against the mesh screen. He is speaking about Kevin, and behind them, their canvas strung chairs, the sound of her brother's steps, the sound of coffee mugs, closing cupboard doors.

'I hope he will go back to university, you know, even if he changes his course. Your mother, she really wants it, but you know would never say it to him. Do you think I should say?'

The smell of the coffee is now filling the porch, the cool dry northern air, as she thinks about her mother who did not ever make the trip north, sitting in the stifling summer night, with her sister Mary, in the near dark, their voices buried in the whir of the electric fan. Her smooth fingers she can almost see in her mind, thin yet strong, which have so cleanly and finely sliced the cucumbers, the smell of early evening, five o'clock sunlight, five o'clock winter dark warmed by a bright kitchen bulb.

Inside the cottage, Kevin catches the sound of his father's voice: 'Kevin,' he hears his father saying.

The bread, five slices toasted and cut on the diagonal, Kevin has readied onto the plate, spread with butter and jam. The coffee, three mugs of it, he'd filled so carefully with a ladle from the saucepan is so hot, the steam is rising, will soon head into the night porch air.

'Kevin,' Sue calls.

'Kevin,' his mother says, as she looks up at him, holding his left hand to her cheek.

It is precisely here that he is disturbed, and that he is also surprised. For he feels the weight of all their voices as they come to him no louder than the thin volume of a distant TV. He loves them. But if this is so, why does he feel so much alone, and why, he wonders, does he know he wants it this way, his life, a lake without trailing voices, wants not the calls which echo within his heart, wants only the silence, that is all.

The cottage is once again behind me, up above me. My heavy-tread boots scuff up the sandy portions of the path leading down to the lake. All the hunters have gone home for the fall. I can see in the bright midday sun, for the sky is beautifully clear, the pink-gray rockface which feels as familiar as family, their characters which one knows through unconscious connection, knows their quiet wants, their sense of humour.

I am quick down this path, but that is not to say I travel without weight. I think how much I would like to be able to write down what I feel at this shore, the intimacies and knowledge that is family, the words whose thickness I feel in my hands as I start rowing out once again. Well, can you? I ask myself, while I ready the oars.

And I know the return of this inside my body, wondering what drives insistence, how I am so uneasy yet, wrists tensed with oars, the direction in view, calm and almost windless before me. Can I ever have that strength of navigation that was knowledge in the body, my father's, when he took us out on the water? It's here that his face fills that space behind my eyes — it is then that he is real, 'he is living, he's with you at this point,' said the Buddhist priest in a service for my dead father. And the words are now a notion, a thin cut in the throat which fills with icy water, which is like invocation for a path, I hear it, its treble at my lips:

'Tell me how to steer, steer the skiff with certainty, in good line, tell me how to make my stroke asssured and easy as if I've done it for years; tell me how to write again in the notebook with the easy proportions and curves which a fine nib and ink describes as evidence, as demands of that wet, the flow to the scratch of paper, moving, moving. Tell me how to work clearly with tireless eye over a keyboard which demands soft touch to play in the current of a screen which lights with the wisdom of alphabets and sentences in aqua against black, figure to ground.'

When she stands there in my eye she is Sue and she is also Hana her mother, is sable and goat brush and wet tidal sand, the aureole contours of a northern sky I see beyond my oars in the break of morning mist; and I know I am coming home, to a rented place, at that. I know such things I ask of the voices have the timbres of man, woman and child, the message for it is of generations that can happen in the arc of a hookwind catching the breath; it is the spawning simile to salmon, salmon in the current, the trailing foam of energy.

Tell me how to watch through this wet glass into the moving luminous Skeena, dark yet opening through the light from this northern country. For here I taste the salt now, over and over, which has permeated the thick dark red strips of salmon roe, the su-zu-ko, into the firm red flesh of the fish, 'shio salmon, shio salmon,' we called it at home, the silver light of the dark Skeena. For here, I taste salt which is memory, and stand upright on the mossy cliff-edge, above a nested jut of the rock, looking out over the lake, eggshells in my hands.

A Holiday Souvenir

Café con leche — with hot milk — café con leche. Café con leche...
café: café: café: café: café: café: café: café: café: café: café con leche,
café con leche... café. Café: café: café con leche. Café: café: café:
café: café: café: café: café: café: café: café: café: café: café: café:
café: café: café: café: café: café.

Café: café con leche he had ordered, was now before him, by his
reclining hand, his eyes wandering through plate-glass windows to
a rather unattractive part of Cordoba. Café con leche... café con
leche — with hot milk — was what he had ordered, it was now
before him, beside his reclining hand, and his gaze was wandering
through plate glass windows, it was a rather unattractive part of
Cordoba. Café con leche... café con leche. At this table, near to the
back end of the retail space, and on the right, the first one on the
right, if one was looking out to the plate-glass shop windows to the
street. Café con leche, the steamed hot milk, seated there, and it,
this part of Cordoba...

The air warm, languidly yeasty with the sweet amber of hot bakery
ovens in the kitchen behind the glossy chrome and marble counters.
Pans of hot water underneath dough doubling in size. His pen,
quickly withdrawn from his valise, and upon the table now; he drank
from his glass. Café: café: café: café: café: café.

The vista to be seen brought no great satisfaction, little cheer indeed to a vacationer's heart: an even stack of apartment buildings of no distinction on the other side of the unadorned sombre avenue, buildings constructed of dull yellow brick; balconies with uniform green awnings — not the wonderful intricacies of black wrought-iron grills of Moorish design, those ornamental features which instantly remind of the local silver filigree, the ring he was now wearing on his third finger and which he had recently purchased from an anxious off-season souvenir shop awaiting the tours. And for all such, this sector of the ancient city conversely held the agreeable dénouement from the emotional pitch of the white lime-washed houses of the Juderìa, the Jewish quarters which lined the narrow, tricky streets taken en route, those ankle-twisting cobbled walks treacherous, insufficiently wide when passing vehicles pressed one sidelong against the calles walls.

The names of calles, the names of grander avenidas and paseos, fingered on a map unfolded to sharp sunlight, which would repeatedly come to tongue: Coronel Casajo, del Gran Capitán, Conde y Luque, Deanes, Isabel II, Cruz Conde, Ambrosio Morales, Palma, Abejar, Almanzor, Encarnacíon, Romeo de Torres, Cabezas.

And yes, what sweet location this was for this rather indecisive winter Sunday, for here at least, it was Cordobans, not tourists, who animated the street; Cordobans in couples or small families, children in tow, dressed in clean pressed clothes, sharp as their eyes and combed hair, light colours or deep primary ones, she would adjust a hair clip, he would unconsciously smooth out a pleat. They came to buy round dark-crusted breads, or little Sunday treats. The four-year-olds would stare.

He himself was eating a dry, sugary bun which with each bite crumbled upon the slick yellow arborite surface of the table. More sugar he stirred into his café. How comfortable this was. He would not budge, certainly not, for the rain had once again started — rain — the days of rainfall in the month of February, the travel brochure had casually, in some margin, informed.

This place he marked with detective eye, pen now in hand, to the trigger: modern chrome and glass — these the display counters and bar, marble and wood; the uniform arborite tabletops; vinyl-upholstered chairs (the colours slid past him); sugary Cordoban apple tarts, such not unlike what he recalled from a dessert after a fine formally presented dinner in the city, some years back. It had been a sugary pie with the odd complication of apple and ham filling. It had been a dry warm evening at a balcony table, fenced to a courtyard below, of oleander, bougainvillea and orange.

O, the tapas! Luscious visits come to a traveller, making a route of the bars, the bodegas. The music of young lean men clapping intricate rhythms in the dark streets and into the passing lights, the tapas. Each day, to purchase the snipped, it is to not sample, but culture, say, an infection of taste, the jiggling plates, the marinated and deep-fried. That is tapas. The delight and grumble, the star and the moody. The small delicious bites: the small plates of the universe. Bar to bar, a cumulative route, eve to eve. Deep-fried squid; peppery green olives; salads of smooth pink fish roe; kidneys softly warmed in sherry; octopus with orange. They are for beer, Morilles, sangria or oloroso. They are economical. Nevertheless, the otherwise carefree visitor must budget the purse's wane, keep the intermittent track, the trail of wet toothpicks and small paper napkins and plates.

A mind which wants the escape of strong food in the mouth plays beyond choice, forever obsessed, never the whitewash of flight, though such culture sends head into reel. The appetite is muscular, plain, necessary, a bell of obligation.

'Must check at train station — the schedule of train departures for Sevilla, posted upon the wall. And there will yes, naturally and of course, there will always be a little time for coffee along the way, ah yes, coffee, at that rather smart café with blue velour chairs, interesting tapas. I am away.'

Always the departures, a train station, no matter where, be the start and be the end, that 'from place to place' never more than a reminder of a burdensome weight, a travel repeated endless times over the body. And so current in the wrist which, a subtle skip in the heart's daily track, you say this of concern, the lodestone on the watch.

'Must check at train station. Posted on the wall of departure times there is, yes, Sevilla, Sevilla, yes and again. And the rather smart café, the interesting tapas, perhaps mussels in pimiento vinagreta. I am away.'

Tapas, whereupon image coincides with bite. The station. It was there, the getting there, there was uh. Insistence: the toy of more; and sad. 'Indeed' in his heart and fathom deep: 'Must check at... '

It was, indeed, yes it was, can still visualize, that hard... the bright. Erect, hard cock, boner, hard-on. The delight of vulgar dark term, the gloom of naming. 'Maa-ma. Paa-pa,' the infant cries, 'round the world. Why the chambers rattle with infant crime. He of course knew his own, that feel in palm, memory, but this, that of the other, that mischievous talon, pink and tuberous, collector. He did not, cannot, escape from sight, that which is not his own, but another's. But always his own for, forever there's an obsession.

The young man is next to him at the urinals, barely a body-width away — their shirtsleeves almost touch, he can feel the intimacies of strength. In his direction, this young man looking, a slight mischievous smile drawing out his gleam, his head turned to the right, his concentrated unswerving stare, natural as guitar. Rubbing, rather quickly, but still gently enough, or perhaps, maybe even methodically, the fingers sliding, sliding, it is practised agitation, beaming.

The tight, constricting bladder, of course, it had brought him here, with no other explanation under the faded sign, that simple fabulous relief (!) he'd thought, 'SERVICIO,' to must, relaxation to the bladder, slowly drawn, relax. At last. And then, yet confronted, the puzzle of action, of another, the muscles of eyes protrude to, the lowly, such infringement, the young man's sharp eyes (must avoid), the youthful fingers, nervous, must avoid eyes of other, and drawn on the plaster wall above where the eyes must retreat to avoid those of the other, the ink stains and letters and his own urine splashing, all is now voiceless and empty, only the two of them now, voiceless into the throat, across the tongue, splashing, spotting his trousers.

Must finish, exit here, and this is the conjugation and the form one most easily learns of the verbs, it, the imperative, is learned at mother's teat (!) and now the search for exit before the jissim of the other, must find the impatient train station line-ups, the departures and arrivals, so drab, so comforting, the smooth metal latch of an official's door.

This taste a malevolent one. No sun again. It was raining. Again that yeasty bakery smell. Sunday café: child gleefully licked a bun iced with dark chocolate. Café con leche, the delicious hot foamed milk he scooped with a spoon — and the dark morose pool, sugary, beneath. 'Where does the day go, where do the days go, these lovely, easy, charming days?'

O, tapas, yes tapas, that's fine. Octopus with oranges, trimmed of their creamy, velvety skin. Hard plates, each day each bodega, lined up side by clattering side, one after the other and dull. And here again trapped, the mind (wrapped in its own habit) within the mouth, not bilious at all, but yet, a sugary residue, a syrupy film to palate, mirror to tongue, with its image of a young man scratched onto the screen, over the plate-glass windows like sign paint. Eyes hot in terminal, Spaniard to outlast any other text or snapshot of Cordoba, the filigree obsession grabbing the third finger with the smell of frankincense in the cool hollow vacancies of yellow-stone churches emptied and echoing of the holy, a single word.

He will rub the pumice, be satisfied like that, the muscles relaxing in the hot tub, the heels made clean, the flesh now smooth as a film drifts upon the water.

'What did he look like — this young man? His complexion? Length of hair? At least the colour of hair remembered, at least. This young man.' He thinks he recalls yellow, a striking yellow: a nylon jacket, a zipper, no, maybe a drawstring.

And all day to wander a single cathedral, trailing the shifting prismatic light designing the stone floors in the shape of iron-grated windows, following as if the perfume of a young woman's callused heels, the echoing yellow light of fading paint. This canvas in this corner is this colour... And in this canvas, the shape of windows and their grates, making a cross, it is so stupidly humorous, the draping light is the draping skein of angelic robe, the draping of paint...

'You yet have your passport, what is the harm, a little inconvenience. That is all. So?' The voice is one abrupt, cuts short, is snapping wrought iron, latch of an official's door.

'What did he look like?' the police official, fingering a red rubber band, demands of the young woman. His linen suit of a pewter colour is wrinkled and stylish. He strides smoothly. The suit designed in the north, in the Catalan, Barcelona. 'And there were a number of men this evening. This is confirmed.' His dark right eye catches the tingle of sun as smartly as does his hair, shiny, precisely combed, of a certain easy class, though once poor in the sierra.

And later, past the customary points, there is humiliation at play in the probing hands of this fellow. 'It was very hot that evening... You are not unfamiliar in the bars of this quarter. And your usual manner of dress...

'They say,... well, to the point: you do not always wear an under-garment beneath your dress. Well?'

'It was you was it not, who approached?' the magistrate has asked.

'And, it is you who advances, once outside. Stop me if you disagree.'

'... so you move your legs, position yourself...'

'... the strap of your brassiere...'

And she is silent though her mouth opens abruptly as if to speak, at this, at this her lips, they are painted a smart colour of red brick as she can only but smile with mockery, the judge a sharply trimmed photograph, contentment quickly filling this room.

And then, stopping the waiter passing by for a fresh glass and another one of those on his tray, the magistrate moves on, for he has managed to spot through the partying crowd, an acquaintance, a local importer of textiles. They chat. The music is Ravel. The trays now hold, incidentally, slivers of Norwegian salmon, delicately smoked.

But it is back there, '... the strap of your brassiere...'

'No, it is not so. No.' Her words have little volume, yet hang in this air...

And then, seated aimless in the usual bar, there is a troubling sensation, finger circling the rim of the stemmed glass; it is a sweet and bitter anise-scented cocktail as young men are clapping the intricate rhythms like Moorish mosaic design in the fading morning dark unslept in. It is the dull pain, recurrent, the search of the shoulder bag for a receipt, a note — when a taxi arrives directly in front, the driver invitingly opens the passenger door...

'Servicio,' the Spanish word for toilet. Water covers the floor. Rough, functional toilet papers, the kind to abrasively agitate the membrane walls of the rectum — these strewn on the wet floor; the canister for these papers is empty. From the taps, both taps, cold water to refresh the hands; perhaps one could at least, wet the mouth, at least. But he would never drink, that kind of plain advice. The words scratched, inked into the wall, which pull at the corners of the lips, are in a Spanish he cannot comprehend, though he of course knows how they speak in the movements of translation into speech, the vulgarity of membrane, a filmy and scratched, sultry tongue. He does not like the way his mind in this instant is as camera, insistent with little self-control. So much is automatic, autodidactic, framed to the gutter in the every movement of waking lives. So much humiliation. So much tongue.

He will see him one day, a convenient, possibly wishful prediction on his part, as if in his cellar a particularly good vintage laid down.

It is the Casa Rubio on the Puerta de Almanzor, where a short thick man, with little hair, white shirt, serves him from the spigot. He takes a second generous sip, wipes his mouth. It is coarse paper saved from a toilet booth. 'Calamares fritos!' he will call out for the sweet pungent taste of sea and very hot oil. His cigarette is burning unattended — for half a minute, before it is resumed. In that interval, he notices, next to him, standing next to him, though shirtsleeves really do not graze, as it was, the two of them in the station.

He is beautiful, this young man. He now sees this 'in the truth,' the filter tip snipped, in the deep revealing light of the bodega. It is wrong, he thinks, to say he has either features or carriage, delicate, effeminate. He is so much the masculine, yet enough gentle. He draws again the smoke against his throat. He looks to the arched doorway, filled with hard white light, throw of contrast to the eyes. In the tidy back kitchen the women cook with hot oil.

First one bite, then another of the tapas, the calamares — these are exceptionally good ones, obviously cooked very quickly in the oil. Distraction swings about the room with its scent, or more precisely, its perfume, a flavour, its visual arrangement. And rather as an afterthought, and it is not a daily insistence at all, there is the swing of desire, the wild persistence for the sensation, into the firm hand's grasp, violently, though to the recreational limit, demanding attention, now teasing the warm pliant palm; then that final direct release, the agonized purity from the fine cultured rhythm of delay, of fingernail edge, of restraint. And upon a finger of this careful hand, the jewel, the silver maze of filigree to his ring, with so many aggressive edges scoring the satisfactory cadence.

He touches at the corners of the eyes, there are tears which he says to himself, 'it is the heat, the sweat,' and through this screen he sees the young Spaniard's right hand turn over, the white cultured pearls, five of them in the soft palm.

He wants like I do want, he thinks. And then, I did not see him to the end, it was, I cannot erase, the taint of bleach in the nostrils, the final spurt, fixing the nasal hairs, drying as flakes of mucus. And yet, he fingers an abhorrence such distaste, his imagination planted against the background of his watch, it is back at the station, again the wet washroom floor, regenerates the smell, alas, the art of cuisine is fantasy! Are there ways to accept the delicious as this, ways to accept the hard season to throat, ways to accept another's remarkable fingers or steely, proficient eyes? We say, 'luscious.' We do, do we not, glue our eyes to glossy magazines filled with the best young women and men barely clothed, do we not call up our mental stratagems to organize recipes into colourful, odorous platters, into a sequence for feasts of seductive conversation with our best friends? We sit with our diversions in hand, charmed by the glowing fire. We clink our glasses together, 'Your health!' we smile to one another.

His eyes wander the clean edges of crime. The insistence is camera, relentless image, steel staples, hanging from pages. This pursuit, about all that a cover story can tell; about soft, inordinately beautiful, child-like women, legs spread over glossy metallic-coloured pages which give off odour to the pressure of fingers, the sweet-sour of damp pages pressed when they are piled. And then, he moves his face across the cleanly cut fibres of sheer nylon.

Across the hardwood floor of the court chamber, black shoes, meticulously polished, newly nailed leather heels, the click-click, the papers carefully piled, the red rubber band of the police official, the echo of heels coming to rest. The smell is now of a very good cologne.

Alone on his back, the firm, rolled pillow crooks his neck to a good slightly arched angle. Her voice on the receiver is lovely, melodious, soft... 'And now, I'm letting down the strap of my brassiere,' she sighs, rather convincingly, he thinks.

'I've nothing beneath my yellow skirt, and you see, I, I move my legs. Listen.'

Between his own bared limbs which press faint stains of perspiration, his eyes are wide open, planted upon a white spot the light bulb fixes to the dark ceiling. And intermittently, other hues, spots of burning glamour enter the retinal accumulation, composing a fleeting puzzle. He is overcome by the smell of the light.

He pulls the damp telephone cord gently from beneath his body, his head sways four centimetres to the right, eyes drop. The ring on his finger, his silver tourist prize and once cool, is now pleasantly warm with the gentle flow of blood and insistence, a ring smoothly polished, coincident with his tightened flesh, the hard argument (of the defendant in counterclaim), his memory which recoils to the whitewash of lime, the narrow twisting streets.

It was still Sunday. A young black-eyed girl of four, maybe five, she was wearing a pale yellow sundress, held a sugary bun wrapped in a paper napkin in her hand. 'Paa-pa,' she cooed. In the cradled centre of his spoon, with which he'd tasted the steamed foamy milk, a ring had stained, as if with the ink of his pen. Outside, where he watched the dull yellow brick of the apartments, built without iron balconies, the rain had begun to subside, but was, for the time being, defeating. Here he remained.

And the tapas is the trail of desire. His ear pressed to the phone in the siesta heat. And yet, he feels all so pleasant, fanned by a breeze through the nylon sheers at the open window; and yet, he relaxes in afternoon repose, under oleander, small oranges and palm, where he is protected from the scarring daylight and heat by the latch on a gate of intricate wrought iron, and the clean soap of rain-washed tiles, the dusky simple melody of a hidden Moorish patio.

The Buddhist Shrine of Battersea Park

There are, in London's Battersea Park, on Prince of Wales Drive and not far from the Albert Bridge, four enormous statues of the Buddha.

The statues form the centre of The Peace Pagoda, a magnificent Buddhist shrine built by a community of Buddhists, one of several they have constructed around the world, dedicated to peace. The facts and figures about the shrine are impressive, and they are detailed at the base.

What follows is an excerpt from the text of that plaque:

The Peace Pagoda was completed in May 1985 as a gift from the late Venerable Nichidatsu Fuji and his Buddhist Order Nippon-zan Myohoji, Japan. Designed by Dr. Oōka, it stands 33.5 metres high and was built by a team including monks and nuns in less than 11 months.

It is the 70th pagoda the Order has built around the world to promote world peace.

It is constructed of Portland stone slabs and the timber is extremely old Canadian Douglas Fir. The roof tiles, of clay, are from Japan.

The kota at the top pinnacle is gilded together with the wind-bells at the octagonal roof corners. The statues are also gilded.

The four positions of the Buddha present various stages of the
Buddha's life.
South: depicts birth at Lumbini, Himalayas
'The universal worship and reverence of the sacred religion
of Buddhism.'
North: depicts Buddha's first sermon
'.........'
East: depicts Enlightenment at Buddhagaya
'Will make tranquil this dream of mine.'
West: depicts Buddha's passing at Kushinara
. 'The establishment of righteousness to bring peace to nations.'
The gift was accepted by London in Honour of International
Peace Year, 1984.

The first time Steven saw the pagoda was on a rush trip he had made
to see a young woman. Her name was Wendy and he'd met her only
a month before in the town of Gramat, in the valley of the River
Lot in southwest France.

One evening, he'd strolled to the local café, the Palais des
Glaces. In Gramat's central square there were two cafés which
competed for clients. The other was the Café des Sports. Steven
patronized both, the less busy one when he wanted solitude, or the
other if he'd become down-spirited after a gloomy restaurant meal
or the weather had not been so bright. The Café des Sports was
busy by turns, dependent on a football game on the TV or men
playing boules outside on the dusty square. The Palais, the Palace
of Ice Cream, a glacier and most au courant, at least in appearance,
of the two, had traded in its '80s faux marble tabletops for those of
dark black and still smarter. It even had cobalt blue. It had installed
a halogen light or two. The ice-cream sundaes which Steven never

ordered were glorious and tempting, beautiful monuments of excess with lit sparklers on top, brought to the table electric and exciting.

The Palais consequently attracted the young of Gramat, with its hot backbeat of tunes by Mauranne or France Gall — this latter who always brought to mind Gramat, for Steven had first heard Gall's hit Babacar in the local Casino Supermarket some years before. It was here at the Palais, he sat down (he'd first scanned the terrace) positioning himself beside two young blonde women engaged deeply in converstion.

As soon as he sat down he heard English, English English, and immediately he thought how they indeed looked so and he was disappointed. Yet short minutes afterwards, when one of them — Cath — had smiled at him — he clumsily joined in the talk which, though not profound, was ideally lighthearted.

Through the afternoon, he had been feverish, and now the evening, in spite of his feeling faint, was glorious. The women were pretty, they spoke English and they spoke even of slight things in a tone and demeanour rich with intelligence and gentleness. They were English tourists in France, but that different sort.

'The people in town are a bit conservative, but they are kind once they recognize you,' said Wendy. 'You can trust them — I've never had a problem.'

It might have been a cliché, yet to Steven, coming from either of his two companions, it was true and to the point. And Wendy laughed rather self-deprecatingly, acknowledging the banality, and Cath joined in.

'One year I'll learn to speak French properly,' Wendy said. 'How wonderful that you speak it so well, Steven.'

At one point Steven silently congratulated himself on having chosen rightly this café with its company, and then they'd been talking almost two hours.

'My God, we've been here almost three hours,' said Cath, looking to Wendy.

'Well, if you are coming to London Steven,' Wendy said, 'that will be nice. I shall have returned by then. Do ring me. I'm in Battersea.'

He lay in his bed by the open window of the hotel room overlooking a now quiet Gramat — quiet except for the occasional high revving of mobylettes from the town centre. 'For sure,' he'd answered Wendy, and he felt excited by the prospect. He recalled London, the pub World's End on the King's Road, greasy but good fish and chips he'd once eaten near there, outside, sitting on a concrete post among parked cars. Nearby was Battersea.

He would definitely ring, and he'd sounded so Canadian, the Canadian English like they sounded English English, and it was comfortable. And then he'd felt sad at that moment. He was leaving the next morning, leaving Wendy and Cath behind.

The next day, he awoke early for a train at dawn, the sound of starlings outside the window which faced Gramat's central square. A hazy band of early rose light passed through the window to a dresser in the corner to his left. He barely recalled the noise of mobylettes he'd fallen asleep to the night before.

As he left the key dangling in his hotel room door, he thought how foolish he was to leave his new English friends, most particularly Wendy. But then he would see her in London, and to remain in Gramat would be an embarrassment of explanations.

A month later, when he arrived in London to stay with his friend Marian, who'd moved there from Canada, he called Wendy. It was the first thing he did. On the other line came Wendy's answering machine. Four days later, they went to the West End together. How much fun it was, the latest play by Stoppard... especially seeing Paul Eddington, the star of the popular English sitcom Yes, Minister.

Afterwards, Wendy had hauled Steven off, literally taken him sweetly by the hand to a crêperie on the King's Road. Rather than a leisurely evening to be dreamed, it seemed all so rushed, for soon they were saying goodnight.

As they headed into the tube station at Sloan Square, her sheer pink scarf tossed loosely around her neck, her baggy navy raincoat blowing in the late August night.

'Steven, I hope it's not rude. But David, my friend (she emphasized this in a pointed tone) is coming to spend the night. He's doing DocPhil at Cambridge. I just found out this evening.'

Steven's face twisted, but not excessively, disappointed but demonstratively forgiving. 'Oh, that's okay.'

'No, it isn't, especially after how we had such a nice talk in Gramat. And me asking you to ring me. It won't always be this way. You are sweet.'

As he rode the Tube north towards Marian's he thought Wendy had looked rather sad. Her face had seemed much more sombre out of the twilight of the French Midi. Of course, she still remained brown from the sun, and her blue eyes held a still, calming focus. She had spoken of her father who had been a playwright. Two plays had been produced, but he had lived mainly as a journalist. He'd died only two years before.

'Father was a good journalist, but he really hated it during his last years. He loved the theatre, but. Do you know, he was a Fabian

Socialist? Active in politics just after the war. He came from Wales, near Swansea. His father was a miner and so were three of his brothers. He went to university. In a poor working-class Welsh family, the aim was that at least one child — son I guess, would go to university. He never forgot that — that's why he was a Fabian. Me, I'm not really interested. Well, maybe it's somewhat parallel, but spiritual things have more been my concern. I have been meditating for a number of years. And now I do my chanting.'

It was extraordinary to Stephen how, even in the rushed talk over crêpes — he'd barely tasted the 'Florentine' of his crêpes — they had shared quickly, intimately. And then, she had mentioned her friend David.

Still, he embraced her gently and formally as they walked towards the Tube.

'He really knew theatre. He never was a critic for the daily he worked for although he would have been splendid, I'm sure. When he died, we, Mum and I, looked through all his unproduced plays in his study in the family cottage in Afriston. We read them before burning them. He'd requested that. Still, it was hard to do — we had a family conference one evening, at the cottage. But then, well...'

And what had Steven talked about through the evening? When they'd met in the West End pub before the theatre, he spent not a few minutes recounting how he'd been so regretful about leaving Gramat, not knowing whether he'd ever see Wendy — and Cath, again.

And then she nudged him, 'And, and...'

'Oh, of course, Steven, you would. I think you realized just as well as I did that time that well, we'll be talking like this when we're both a bit longer in the tooth. Didn't you? Don't you?'

He'd gone over in some detail, though not excessively, his trip, the 'awful six hours on the train to Paris. First the change at Brive, then another at Poitiers.' It had been hot, he'd been burning up, and his head had throbbed. He could find only one position in which the throbbing was marginally more 'tolerable,' if that could be said. The smell of sandwiches — they were Spanish people with very strong garlicky orangey ham — had made his head spin.

'Poor dear,' Wendy had said. 'You should've stayed in Gramat. Cath and I would have brought you up to the house. Fed you Provençal herbs tisanes and honey. Next time, my sweet boy.'

'It was incredible, though, Wendy, when I got to Paris. As it got in, the train... Gare d'Austerlitz, I almost felt as if I was coming home. The last couple of times I've been, Paris has felt like home to me.'

'I could live there,' she said. 'Some people just hate it. Oh, the people, I guess, is what they seem to talk about. But I've never had an unpleasant experience with Parisiens. Nothing like Londoners...'

It was always good to hear positive things about Paris and Parisiens. Except for one evening when a young man in a café near Pigalle took in Steven's Asian features, sneered at him, went on about Cambodiens, Steven had only felt charmed by Parisiens. He defended them to the point of exaggeration.

'My friends in Paris, most who've always lived there — they say they hate it and then love it — at the same time. That's why they leave when they get upset or stressed out. Out to the country.'

'Le Weekend,' said Wendy.

'I kind of felt that... there I was in Gare d'Austerlitz, and, and they do always come back to Paris refreshed... so I was in Austerlitz and thought, aha, I'm cured. I slung my bag over my shoulder and it felt so good, marching past, there's that row of shops which sell cameras, watches and stereos and things. There's a great place too for wine and some pretty good food, where they sell it.'

'You mean that place which sells the tinned patés, confit and things? Very good place for rillettes.' She laughed with just a hint of delay. He did, too, after her expression turned her words toney.

'I'm serious, really, I love rillettes.' They laughed again.

'So do I, I'm an "amateur" of the cuisine of the Sud-ouest.'

He visualized the row of brasseries which face the station, their faux marble tables, the chairs all facing the street. At any time of day, tourists or travellers waiting for train connections to other destinations would choose one of these venues or the next — or the next. They would sip their coffees or draft beers. Others would be heartily eating their choice from the set formula menu loudly displayed — crudités, marinated herring with warm potatoes, preserved duck leg, maybe steak frites. 'De la Gare...' — they were so typical. It could be anywhere, a town of any decent size in France.

'I went to a place that had a menu for 60 francs — supposedly Auvergnat — but I just stood at the bar with an espresso. My head was more dizzy, you know, with the pinballs, noise. Not like on the train — those Spanish sausage smells on the train. Euchgh.'

'Well, I got home and guess what — my fever got worse that night. It was freezing in Paris. What was it in Gramat? Thirty-four degrees or something?'

His feelings still clung to the past, that one London evening. It had followed him back to Paris. 'God, I just kept talking on and on about that. Phew.' And had he said anything that evening, anything of well... substance, when Wendy had been so intimate, intimate as if seeking response as she spoke frankly about her father?

What an impression he must have left on his London visit. He had had virtually nothing to say.

In front of him were the first pages of his Paris telephone directory, directions for dialling long distance, country code, local codes, etcetera. After crossing the English Channel, he'd boarded the train at Dieppe in bright midday. By late afternoon he was lugging his bag past the magazine stands in Gard du Nord in the depressing 10th arrondissement.

Gare du Nord was not Gare d'Austerlitz, it was the station always so much otherly European and unLatin, those arriving from Britain, the young backpackers searching for lockers, the transients in dirty navy blue suits, dusty heel-worn shoes, the smells of urine when you turned a corner looking for the Métro, so unlike Gare d'Austerlitz which pointed to the Midi and Spain. When the train had arrived in Gare du Nord, he'd become perturbed by the last phone call with Wendy, agitated with himself, agitated with the young travellers, loud, jockeying, or sleeping on the floors of the station.

He finally dialled — all the way through the numbers — he was nervous and concerned, the click and cheery voice of Wendy on the other end almost too quick. Outside his window, the market on rue Mouffetard was opening up for the afternoon. The smells of roast chicken, the tarragon, the thyme, from the butcher down the street. The yelling between merchants, good-natured, clichéd.

The last time they'd spoken had also been by phone. ('Call me before you leave London, Steven. I am sorry about this, David coming.') He especially remembered her 'Please,' and then the pink scarf against the calf-length navy blue coat heading down the stairs.

It had been rather disturbing, but also interesting, to discover how much he carried his feelings on his face, how, as Marian had told him, his face always twisted like a child's with his emotions. It had been comforting to talk to Marian back in her London flat, for she knew him well, questioned him after that last call to Wendy. He let it out in short remarks — someone, he didn't mention Wendy by name, she was an illustrator, it was an instant closeness though not romantic. But after the call he'd understood Wendy's manner, the cheer barely concealing the grim, she was going for more tests, it was serious, but she didn't say more, and he didn't ask more.

She was concerned, 'But,' she said. He could hear the smile, the generosity in the upward lilt to Wendy's tone. 'Well, Steven, I thought well, it seemed important to tell you... that if I was a bit out of sorts.'

'Not the best time to go back home, eh, Marian? Maybe I'll come back to London before I head to T.O.'

'You're crazy Steven.' He was always charmed by Marian's sweetness and gentle decorum. 'You most certainly can stay here if you do return. It would be nice to have you. Chez toi, okay?'

Now, two weeks after leaving London, and still Wendy did not know the results. She seemed no different as he spoke to her — the same cheery voice, yet not out of proportion to the truth, the anxiety.

'Wendy, maybe I'll come to London, just for a short visit, a day.'

She sounded surprised, naturally. 'That'd be lovely, but it's quite a trip. You have the 'sous,' Steven? Really.'

He could not detect any signals in her words or tone. 'I have just enough money left. Besides. Well, since I'm here across the Atlantic and all. I don't know when I'll be back again. It's just that.

It's worth it, friendship... it isn't often you meet someone you get like this with...'

'Ah, yes, I think I heard this the last time, about leaving Gramat.'

Yet, without definite signal, in ambiguity, he confirmed his visit, his folly. 'Right. By Battersea Park,' he said. 'I probably told you about the fish 'n' chips, uh. Anyway.' His face was flushed. He put the receiver down, slightly trembling, grinning. It would be good, the trip. He would see Wendy, they would talk, he'd find out, he hoped, more about her illness, it was maybe what she wanted, he would wish her well, he would quick it back to Paris. A week later, he'd be in Toronto.

A few days later he was there in Victoria Station, digging out his old London tourist map from his shoulder bag, digging out his blue pocket address book. Over the Albert Bridge, a bus could take him to Prince of Wales Drive. Minutes later he recalled that mild evening in Gramat as he sat in one of the several sandwich shops across from Victoria Station.

When he found her flat (which took longer than estimated, for he'd been somewhat mistaken about the location), he ran up the stairs to the third floor. She was already waiting, the door open, all light and bright, even though the day was overcast. One of those thick muggy London days in August.

'Bonjour,' he saluted. She smiled, gave him two quick kisses before he could.

'Coffee, Steven?'

'How about, uh, tisane,' he said, 'with honey — from a sunny clime. No, coffee would be wonderful.'

She grinned softly to his small joke. 'Café crème, un grand. My special, I froth up the milk in the blender.'

'Well, I don't believe this,' he said. 'So, what's on the agenda?' Wendy smiled gently, her cheeks and eyes pulling together. 'Not that I mind, we could just sit here.'

They sat with coffee for about thirty minutes, but then she was off for an appointment she could not break. His visit had been, after all, hastily finalized, nevertheless she profusely apologized.

'That's okay,' he said, 'but it's too bad.' She was scurrying, calling out from the washroom, brushing her hair. 'But it's too bad,' he repeated more loudly, 'eh?'

For two hours that morning Steven wandered about the neighbourhood, waiting. She'd left him a set of keys to come and go as he pleased. He looked for the chip shop by World's End, but could not find it. In fact, he was to later discover, it was over the Thames, the Albert Bridge. Around the corner from Wendy's flat was a Bretonne crêperie. He lunched there on crêpe Florentine 'for old times' sake.'

Back at the flat, he browsed through her books. The light was even brighter, white, the flat sparsely and simply decorated. A large window was open, the flat had a breezy tropical feel. A photo of Wendy was on a low glass-topped rattan table — her hair long but tied up — tanned even more than she'd been in the Midi. Her arm was wrapped around a small beaming Thai woman dressed in a business suit.

There were not many books, two small shelves, a couple of thriller bestsellers, cookbooks, a book on France, others. At least half were various Buddhist texts. One, a small mustard-coloured chapbook handbound with thread, was by an organization called Nichiren Shoshu, England.

He was leafing through it when she returned.

'Oh,' she said, surprised.

The first mention of this chapbook came, not at his probing, when they went for a walk that afternoon.

'I've been going there for about two years,' she said as they crossed the street towards Battersea Park. She put her hands around his left arm, held him firmly without pressure, as if they'd done it for years, walking like this, talking. It had been just after her trip to Thailand that she'd begun chanting.

'It was quite a trip for us — David... maybe more for me, but. I've been all over the continent, father believed in letting us travel alone even as children, but Thailand was remarkable.'

'Have you ever seen The Peace Pagoda here, Steven?'

In fact, through all his London trips, he had never really been to Battersea Park.

'I love it. I feel so grateful to be living so close to it. You must imagine, some days when I'm not in the best of sorts... I can come here. It was built by an order of Buddhists to commemorate the Year of Peace. They've built them all over the world. We are very fortunate that they thought highly enough of London and of Battersea.'

That evening they would have dinner together. A friend of hers, a close friend, Laurie, would be joining them, something that had been planned in advance, had been put off a couple of times. He agreed that it would be all right, he would find her smashing, she thought.

The pagoda was beautiful, as Wendy had said. He couldn't at first fathom the size of it as they climbed up the steps and looked out from the platform towards the Chelsea Embankment of the River Thames. He was too taken by the kind of serene yet proper mannered charm of Wendy, an attractive strength.

She was quiet much of the time now as they wandered and now again were wandering the perimeters of the pagoda. She would hold his arm without moving her hand except for the occasional pressure. 'I've found a friend for — until we're long in the tooth,' blurted Steven, carefree with the cliché. She released her hold at this, looked at him with mock pain. She then walked by his side, not touching, but certainly this did not matter, and they continued.

He stood at the bottom of the pagoda and the image was quite unbelievable, an image in which he placed himself as viewer over the golden faces of the Buddha in the middle of London. Wendy, her loose wide-legged white pants a few inches above her ankles, a baggy mint green thin cotton-knit pullover, a camera held up to her face taking his picture. He held up his camera, too, trying to get in part of the statues, their golden shine, Wendy, and the crazy spectre of the bannered festive Albert Bridge over the Thames. There was too much light in the viewer, he thought, the photo would be developed, a rosy-orange band of over-exposure at the side. But what did it matter? He snapped.

'When we met in Gramat and you talked about visiting, I immediately thought that I wanted to share this, the pagoda, with you. I don't know why I didn't suggest it the first time.'

It was just after this that they turned towards the entrance and Wendy told him about how important she'd found her 'spiritual path' in the last month or so, that she found her life was now really a gift. Every day was a revelation, was like the opening of a gate.

And there she could chant, it was as if a flower had unfurled to light, she saw all David gave to her, saw the fragility and relative smallness of her own life, her hardships. This filled her with strength. And even though David did not share this spiritual inclination, it was in such a situation they found their lives had converged, they reforti-fied each other.

'It's the kind of thing I sense,' she said, 'like with you in Gramat, and today with you, the way you've come here. You're very gener-ous, Steven.'

She talked about the tests. She'd noticed something and imme-diately had gone to her doctor to examine the swelling, thickness. He'd shown her the x-ray, pointing with his pencil, following the shadowy image set against the screen of light. Stephen averted his eyes towards Wendy's shoulders. She shrugged and then became silent.

It was not, it seemed, that she wanted to be evasive, secretive. Her comments simply were general, but precise. Clearly she wanted to say these things she said, this opportunity with Steven.

Mainly she pointed to how things had at once come together. The health problem just at the point of her contentment in com-mitting to the arduous Nichiren route. Whatever happened to her life, she was in a better position to deal with things than any time previous. A strength, the power of others chanting, the common direction of energy.

Dinner with her friend Laurie was lovely, though not so much like he wished, not so much like the miraculous afternoon, for it was not, it was evening. Yet it was the sense of passing time — at her flat, Battersea and the pagoda, then at the table, hours together, he counted them in his head. At Laurie and Wendy's suggestion they ate at the same crêperie he'd lunched at, though Steven did not say.

Laurie was indeed engaging, full of life, not so much like Wendy, he found her more Canadian, North American in a way. She spoke more openly, sat casually, hunched over the table, head bobbing as she talked, and Wendy too became more lively, playful. They laughed, the three of them together. 'We're rather alike, Laurie and I.'

'A lot of people think we're sisters,' Laurie said. 'Don't you think, Steven?'

What had returned Steven to recollections of that dinner coversation was a newspaper. It was five years later.

Across from him, the newspaper the young woman was reading gave Steven motive to speak. The words on the masthead, a name full of nostalgia, in Battersea: Nichiren Shoshu, England.

Steven and Wendy had returned to the flat after walking Laurie to the Tube. They had talked again though, but for an hour. She'd poured two snifters of Armagnac, good Armagnac which caught his romantic fancy.

Across from him, the young woman had now set aside her paper. Was he, too, descending the train at Norwich?

'Yes,' Steven said, 'but I'm changing there. I'm going out to Beccles to visit a friend. My friend Joanna.'

'It's just super out there,' she said. 'The beach near Southwold is smashing.'

Over the Armagnac, the talk had changed once more. No longer talk of Buddhism, but again of her father's plays. He'd spoken about his attachments to his family, the family house in Toronto. Wonderful forsythia bush out front, the lilies of the valley out back. And now, briefly, Battersea, its formal gardens came to mind, the train continuing northward.

'I've always wanted that,' Wendy had said, 'to find perfume that smelled of that — or freesia — just the natural flower scent, but I've never been successful.'

He'd playfully suggested Grasse, Provence.

'France,' she sighed.

'D'accord,' Steven had agreed, holding and swirling the Armagnac in his mouth before swallowing.

His flight had been very early, he would get himself up from the fold-out, use Wendy's alarm. She had not awakened to say goodbye, but he'd hoped she'd offer. He let himself out quietly, in the dark, whispering, "Bye, Wendy,' so only he could hear. The door had slightly slammed to his pull.

'I'm chanting every day right now,' the young woman said, handing Steven the newspaper so he could look. 'I've just returned from a youth conference. If your friend is still in London, I'm certain she would have been there.'

'You can keep the newspaper. Uh, oh yes,' she dug into her shoulder bag, then extended her hand. 'Take this, I found it on the beach at Southwold.'

It was a small flat round gray stone. In the middle was a perfect round hole.

'It's good luck,' she said. 'Call me if you want — on your way back to London. Remember, my name's Joanna. Smithers, only Smithers in town. Nam Myoho Renge Kyo.'

It was how Wendy had ended her letters. 'Nam Myoho Renge

Kyo.' 'I'm sure we'll be in touch until we're long in the tooth,' she'd said. 'Nam Myoho Renge Kyo.' He remembered this about Wendy and their mutual conviction, now the years passing.

After his return to Toronto it was he who had first written. Wendy had responded almost immediately (it was surprising how fast mail travelled between Toronto and England). They had been letters not long-winded, barely a page and a half, but clear and ample, words passed between familiar friends. Once he'd phoned and she said the doctor was pleased but wanted to see what would happen in a few months. It was important that she was strong, looked after herself. Steven did not pry.

'For heaven's sake, Steven, this is costing you a lot,' she said.

'Yeah, I guess, we better say goodbye,' and they had hung up.

It was then Wendy who had written. It had been just a quick note on rough rice paper (handmade, he noticed with delight, in the Cotswolds). She and David had gone 'bonkers,' decided on a last-minute 'bucket-flight' to Thailand. 'I'll write you from there,' she promised. There had been a Bangkok address. He had faintly recalled the woman in the business suit, or perhaps a sense of, back in time.

'We are well,' she wrote. 'I feel very strong. My health is first-rate. I'm chanting often. Someday would like to live here. People are so wonderful, always smiling. Even POLICE! Did you notice the photo, by the way, in my flat?'

The image of the small Thai woman. It had been so clear.

'As to the flat, Steven, had to give it up. I will send you a note as to my whereabouts in London. As for now, I'm in PARADISE. Do write...'

He felt the sense of sitting there, Armagnac in hand, a nostalgia. He'd never be in that flat again.

In the end, he had not written, at least not promptly. He'd thought of it, then had become preoccupied in Toronto. A woman barely out of her teens, which had made him almost twice her age. He thought it ridiculous, but pursued it, while only admitting it as friendship. Finally, after a clumsy phone call, they had gone out. They had gone out a second time, that had been it, barely a kiss on the lips, off centre. Then he'd tried to catch up wind, thought of writing, Thailand, Thailand. Given the date, he had figured she would already be long gone from the Bangkok address.

Two letters to London (he assumed they would be forwarded) went unanswered.

The second of these he'd written as a last, asking for contact, for he had been anxious, ('Just let me know you're okay... huh?'), and then, why had she become unresponsive as quickly as they'd become life-long friends? He wrote as much, daring to be frank.

But simply nothing had passed. No more the brief letters, their shared affections for France, the southwest, the French. He wrote to Marian, Marian's where he'd stayed that time in London, had asked her to call Wendy's old phone number. 'Nothing,' she had reported. 'When will you visit again?'

It was not so much the friendship. That she would be alive, in good health, still doing her regular chanting. That Christmas he had gone to Christmas Mass, though he wasn't Christian, to pray for Wendy's health, just to make some religious effort.

At one point he'd thought that she and David had actually stayed in Thailand. Again, the woman in the business suit had become more hazy, a kind of framed shadow beneath the pristine white wall, lost in the immaculate daylight; he'd pictured more easily the green batik print cushion and the small rattan table by the bookshelves. Surely she would have written.

Trailing after — Shannon — he'd forgotten her last name, the twenty-year-old, time, and apparently Wendy had, for him, disappeared. For two weeks leading up to the first time out with the young woman, things had been neglected. When the flirtation abruptly ended, it had taken barely three days to take it in stride, rationalize, comfort self with the silliness of the escapade. He then kept looking at the Thai postcard on his barren desk. All for a kiss, off centre, poor execution.

'Oh, I thought you were an Aquarian, Steven.'

Laurie had said it. They were still waiting for their salads, sipping Fronsac wine.

'My boyfriend Phillip is Aquarian. In the end, Aquarians are consumed by their self, freedom, individuality and all. It's not a criticism. Really. But I don't think he really can commit himself to one person for life. You probably like to think so, but... The universal lovers — the peace-generation types. Uh, religion, spiritual stuff.' She sighed.

'I think it's possible.'

'I don't mean to be hard, Steven,' she smiled.

'Well, I kind of think, seems to me it's worth trying to share kindness with as many people as possible,' Steven said.

'I don't mean kindness. I mean real commitment, trying to love more than you really can.'

'Well, I think that's hard — what's possible, what we can. Seems you, we have to try. We're here to share, that's what I think,' he looked over to Wendy, and she did give, he felt, a silent assent, looking towards Laurie, too.

He couldn't believe he'd talked so, it had been such an embarrassing conversation. And yet the memory totally absorbed him.

'Say, like. I didn't think so, but I know that I now would think about getting married. I wouldn't have before... you know, I did live with someone for a few years, but. We said to each other we could see, go out with others, if we really wanted to? But, now I mean married but at the same time in a kind of relationship where you don't stop sharing and committing to others, nothing to do with romance and sex and all. When you get married, I mean.'

'Laurie, what you're saying has a lot of truth, but I do know Steven well enough that he's genuine, he's got a good heart.'

His instant memory of Laurie was neither unpleasant nor weighty, it was that he still carried the load of that one point made in the Bretonne bistro, both of them not quite agreeing and he defensive, true, but a confusion of feelings of being miscast. It lingered still from that table.

At the bottom end of the map of London was the green of Battersea Park. On the same side of the Thames as The Oval, cricket ground where once he'd spent an afternoon with London friends, they ate 'gateaux' from a Soho patisserie. The map was an old one, typical British Tourist Authority map, he'd folded and unfolded the same for so many years.

When he arrived at Victoria Station from the country, he was gripping the Buddhist newspaper the young woman had given to him on the train. In Beccles, at his friend Joanna's, he'd been moody, rather bad company, a bad guest. The newspaper had brought distraction, had brought Wendy once again into his life, vaulting

him five years backwards. Nichiren Shoshu, Nichiren Shoshu. Nam
Myoho Renge Kyo. It was not Jodo Shinshu, the Pure Land Sect,
the faith of his father and aunt and uncle back in Toronto, the major
sect in Japan. Nichiren Shoshu he knew virtually nothing about.
But it was the thread which tugged with continuity from that brief
charmed time with Wendy.

Finally, as a last try, on his return from Beccles, he phoned Cath,
the same whom he'd met with Wendy in Gramat. At first, she'd been
rather cool — obviously puzzled, and maybe even annoyed.

'Oh, yes, in Gramat. I remember. The Canadian?' The upward
lilt to her voice reminded him of Wendy. And then most stunning,
'Certainly I still see her from time to time,' said Cath. 'I will most
certainly tell her that you asked after her and give her your number.
How long will you be in London then, Steven?' There was no means
of delaying his departure date and time, 11:50 a.m., a day after
tomorrow.

The map of London was an old one. Typical British Tourist Authority map he'd scotched where the folds had torn through. At the
bottom end was the green of Battersea Park. Slightly to the left and
above was the Albert Bridge.

The bus was midpoint upon the Albert Bridge. The banners
finally pulled into range, the composition of the viewfinder, Wendy
holding her camera to the right of the photo. The day was muggy,
but the sun was bright, glaring through London's August afternoon
smog. It was magical. The light had foiled the photo ultimately,
with its band of orange-red over-exposure. Unsuitable to really
show anyone, to enlarge. Send to Wendy, if he knew where. Still
it was magical.

Wendy would still come to The Peace Pagoda if she was in London. Perhaps there was some motive of some chance meeting — and some chance it would be — in Steven's little pilgrimmage, his first to the pagoda since that day with Wendy. It certainly crossed his mind. Five years.

He'd passed through London but briefly since he'd last seen Wendy, but had been mainly preoccupied with meeting friends. Now the way was open to him again. He got off the bus soon after it crossed the bridge, then walked along Prince of Wales Drive. The row of regal buildings rose before him; he could no more easily distinguish Wendy's old flat from the rest and he'd forgotten the address, written on the back pages of an old date book. It was simply, the same street, the same place, around there. He found the park entrance, imagined an instant with her, for it was the same.

But then things became complicated. He did not really know Battersea Park, could not find his route by which Wendy had once led him, fingers wrapped around his arm. It was as if one never knows a visited place where another has carried the map, located the streets, pinpointed the transit stops and restaurants. And that day back then, he'd been excessively charmed and walked lamb-like to her gentle pull and push, firm touch to his arm, and then the Buddha sat before them.

'There it is, Steven. Marvellous, isn't it?'

Eventually he came upon a map post and felt finally more confident about his route. He felt alternatively lost and then found, a grate of emotions. They were of fancy and wish, of tranquility yet desire for such taste and feeling, the Buddha as He sat before them, linked, the café crèmes in the halogen glare of a noisy French glacier, the war statue before them in the town centre of Gramat, one evening. The feeling was odd, appealingly painful.

He could hear the banners of the Albert Bridge, though they were nearly a mile away. The sun was low in the sky, a blue enough pale, it would rapidly closet to violet then black.

It has been warm in the sun, but now its continued presence does nothing to lighten the cool of an autumn evening descent. His pullover is only sufficient. It takes barely ten minutes. It is at the far end of the park. He does not know how he will react to see this. That his mental preparations might or might not alter the view, the cast of dark to the bright that had ultimately tinged effectively the photo. The bright orange bar of light is again in his eyes, now without camera he proceeds, the River Thames somewhere there in the near distance, he proceeds.

There is a pamphlet published by the Tibetan Youth Congress, Canadian Branch, entitled Training The Mind. It is part of a text from a talk some years past by the 14th Dalai Lama of Tibet.

The photo of the Dalai Lama is a full head shot, the top of his balding head cropped and fading into the dark mustard-yellow stock of the two-fold five-page pamphlet. His eyes, behind metal and plastic-rimmed glasses, are focussed with a verbal animation. His head is slightly tilted from his right to his left.

Whether one believes in religion or not, or whether one believes in rebirth or not, there is not anyone who does not appreciate compassion and mercy. Right from the moment of our birth, we are under the care and kindness of our parents. Then, later on in life, when we are oppressed by sickness and become old, we are again dependent on the kindness of others. Since it is the case that at the beginning and end of our lives we are so dependent on others' kindness, how can it be that in the middle we neglect kindness towards others?

This is from page 3. The following is an excerpt from page 4.

When one meets people of unpleasant or unfortunate character, who show a bad disposition towards one, one should not just neglect or discard such people, but generate a sense of even greater kindness towards them.

There are indeed occasions when one has been very kind and helped someone a great deal, and that person should repay one with some feeling of kindness. But instead of displaying kindness, he becomes ungrateful and shows one bad manners and so forth. Now this is a very sad situation indeed, but within the context of the practice of altruism, one should show even greater kindness towards that person, and have a sense of even greater kindness. In Shantideva's 'Engaging in the Bodhisattva's Deeds' a very important thing is said — that someone who acts as an enemy towards one is one's best teacher... Therefore for somebody engaging in the Bodhisattva practices, another person who acts as an enemy is a person who should be treated with tremendous respect.

'We're here to share,' he looked over to Wendy for some assent. He couldn't believe he'd talked so, they had had such an embarrassing conversation.

'I know that now I would consider being married, and still. But at the same time, you should be able to in it, have, you don't stop committing to others. Being married and all, I mean.'

How such burden had defined the meal with its lingering tastes.

'I don't mean kindness. I mean trying to love more than one really can. We just don't have the energy — or one doesn't end up

being able to really give oneself to the relationship. I grant people
believe their intentions, good intentions.'

'So you don't think it's possible then?' he wondered.

'Maybe to the point that it pleases yourself, your own idea of
your self and your principles. But what are our own limits? I mean,
I include myself here.'

Head tilted from his right to his left, eyes behind metal and
plastic-rimmed glasses, his eyes are focussed with verbal animation
upon the dark mustard-yellow of a page, the 14th Dalai Lama.

In the near distance on the same side of the Thames, the parkland
continues. Here one can observe solitary couples (solitary, for they
seem so bachelored even in crowded cafés and shops, unto themselves) and those alone too, jogging and yet more social than those
pairs, all of them like pigeons and crows, they appear, the speed
and form of heads bobbing in gentle turns. Further on, across the
river, rise the towers of The City to the extreme right, and there is,
closer of course, Westminister, St. Paul's, all the usual common
sights which identify London, best described by Michelin in every
language of significance. If Paris has been more a City of Dreams,
from here London is more a city of present desires, solid, ambitious,
the green of trees, the stability of natural lawns, fenced, measured,
projected intentions, lives. In the park, one can too think further
north to Hyde Park, the Serpentine, the gallery there, a pleasant
preoccupation before or after an American-style Sunday brunch.
There is, too, of course Harrod's and all the extraordinary 'food
halls' to which only Fauchon in Paris can compare.

And there to the left is the Albert Bridge, where a stiff wind
blows all the colourful pagentry banners, which at this distance are

silent. In any case, in London it is just the ever-constant hum of traffic, to visitors clearly signified by the Black Top taxis, which motor heavily, with seeming abandon, purposeful in their carriage and those also of their passengers.

Clearly, in front, the sense of tranquil proportions, of a limited yet breathable space, provides a point of overview. Below, if the neck would quite smartly turn, is the route made along the path from the entrance to Battersea's wonderful park; and there to the signpost, upon which is the map, leading just to this spot, this, this spot among several other predetermined itineraries, charted destinations, plans.

The hand takes such comfort on the seeming grainless, well-finished wood, alternatively grips at the railing or then flattens, slides along it, providing with a final swivel of the wrist and push, the leverage required to move fluidly off and turn, take in the sight from the other side of the pagoda, or descend the steps, a foot slaggardly trailing momentarily behind.

One can spend a good deal of time here at the base too, perimetering The Peace Pagoda. For as one tilts head upward, whether angled right or slightly left, there are four different faces, four different poses, capturing the four cardinal points of feeling: and all in the end are the same, each a fragment of each other, yet whole.

The statues form the centre of The Peace Pagoda, a Buddhist shrine built by a community of Buddhists, one of several they have constructed around the world, dedicated to world peace. The facts and figures about the shrine are impressive and detailed at the base.

What follows is an excerpt from the text of that plaque:

The Peace Pagoda
The Peace Pagoda was completed in May 1985 as a gift from the late Venerable Nichidatsu Fuji and his Buddhist Order Nippon-

zan Myohoji, Japan. Designed by Dr. Ōoka, it stands 33.5 metres high and was built by a team including monks and nuns in less than 11 months.

It is the 70th pagoda the Order has built around the world to promote world peace.

It is constructed of Portland stone slabs and the timber is extremely old Canadian Douglas Fir. The roof tiles are from Japan.

The kota at the top pinnacle is gilded together with the wind-bells at the octagonal roof corners. The statues are also gilded.

The four positions of the Buddha present various stages of the Buddha's life.

South: depicts birth at Lumbini, Himalayas

The universal worship and reverence of the sacred religion of   Buddhism.'

North: depicts Buddha's first sermon.

'........'

East: depicts Enlightenment at Buddhagaya

'Will make tranquil this dream of mine.'

West: depicts Buddha's passing at Kushinara

The establishment of righteousness to bring peace to nations.'

The gift was accepted by London in Honour of International Peace Year, 1984.

The first time Steven had seen these statues of the Buddha was on a rush trip he had made to London to see a young woman. Her name was Wendy and he had met her only a month before in Gramat in the valley of the River Lot in southwest France.

It is now a muggy August day as that one some years before, and equally it is not. The light here is soft, though even in the fading sun, the brightness throws a red-orange glare. This, to be exact, in turn gleams with a special soft cast, off the lustrous gold of the shapely round features of each position of the Buddha.

The light is thence captured by the murky waters of the River

Thames, there especially where a bridge, the Albert Bridge, fords the waterway supporting a typical double-decker bus carrying a half-load of riders some who gaze out to the colourful banners blowing fiercely but silently in the wind.

Michiko

Is this the sound I can make?
The voice insists its
wake, the drum inscribes
the shell's shell

   sea of th' inner ear.

And mother-daughter
mother-son
daughter-son
mother's daughter
son's mother
'ton-ton-ton...'

m's d
m's s
  m s d
'ton-ton-ton'
is this the voice
in its wake?

m's   s   d's

   d's   m

m
     d
       s

Now her voice, Gloria's voice, so clear, insistent to her ear. And there, a distant stretch of light arches over, then beyond, to the eastern slope of the mountains over Digby Island, Prince Rupert. It is there, at the small northcoast airport, the airplanes from Vancouver land. Her voice, that of Michiko's eldest daughter, is soft, she listens to it on the phone. And long before Michiko was Gloria's age already she'd become sad, walking with her sister up Gore Avenue, in Vancouver, for their mother had died.

('One day,' Michiko once says to Gloria, 'I run home from school, I was crying. That time I'd taken sugar sandwich for school lunch. I always have this,' she says.

And that day, she explains, she watched her schoolmates eating cheese and ham sandwiches. She remembers being chased by boys who laughed at her, 'not because of my slant-eyes, Nihonjin,' but she never knew why. Yet then in terror, to feel, long after the door closed safely behind her, at once both wrong and the wronged and not know really why. She came home, hands damp with tears to the kitchen, ran to her older sister, but Kane wasn't there, like her mother was now never there. Their mother had died with a fever three years before.)

Michiko looks out over Cow Bay, the black and orange oil tanker docked out there, this view from her room on Borden Street on the hill above the water. Ever since her arrival three days before. This house, once the grand home of a doctor, she remembers, so many years ago now. Cow Bay, where she used to go down by the hotel when she was young; and then Seal Cove, some miles away, to visit her friend Keiko whose mother cooked in the mess hall at the sawmill.

Then those other times too, Vancouver days, days with Kane her older sister, their mother dead.

She had only a few months ago shown her children a photo of herself — a child is just standing, there, it's after the funeral procession for her mother down Powell Street, as it had been, always, Vancouver. They had just finished Saturday night dinner, and Michiko's children were sitting over their coffee at the dining room table, such old BC photos from the sideboard, scattered now over the table.

And then they'd looked, seated around table, hunched over. The photo of Powell Street in the present. A Japanese restaurant which is now there, just the last fifteen years, the sad-looking coffee shop, its skid-row derelicts, the tidy plastic chairs, and then in the distance, on the left, the Japanese fish store of Michiko's second cousin where they made kamoboko and satsu-mage, fishcakes which were shipped out to Japanese food stores in the east.

She thought of Powell Street. Powell Street. Vancouver, she thought of her mother and Kane. Powell Street, the way she still recalled.

('Another time... Father, your grandfather was working in interior, you see. And so he told us that we could be like grown women, not young girls. We, your aunt was twelve, so I was ten. Together, to get along together. Set up house in a flat. He would send us money each month through Yamanaka-san on Powell Street..... And so we got a place on Powell Street on the 300-block.

'It was a good time. When we lived in Vancouver.'

And one time, a year she was living on Nicola Street, all the way along Robson Street, one day she just began to feel sad about her mother, she was playing 'Shi-na-no-yoru' on the harmonica her mother had given her, she was lonely ('ohh, oh my'), she tore off her tunic... but she couldn't cry very long, for she had to do her housework for hakkujin as a 'schoolgirl' ('that time, I was going to Lord Roberts Public School') it was all the way along Robson Street, living on Nicola Street, one time, she just began to feel sad.

'I was so happy with this harmonica. I always kept it in the box. Some days, I would just open the box and look at it, so precious, ne Gloria.')

Michiko stands by the window, the view over Cow Bay, the black and orange oil tanker docked out there, this view from her room on Borden Street. And to the left, just out of view, the swings of the grassy playground where once, sixty years ago, was the public school overlooking Cow Bay, Prince Rupert.

And her daughter's voice is so clear and Michiko tells her, 'Remember, Gloria, when you were in public school? You would come and say to me after school, "Mama, I could eat those sugar and butter sandwiches every day." And your friends wanted them, too.'

And she is on the phone, Michiko's hand still smooth, soft, the very fine wrinkles, the light sheen of hand cream, roses, rose petals, phone pressed to ear, the arch of light further and further over the northcoast mountains, Digby Island. Prince Rupert.

Michiko now seventy, exactly, has come here by herself from Toronto to see Prince Rupert once more, never before has she been in an airplane. And she will stay the summer, see Keiko's stepdaughter, the last Kadonaga family still in Rupert, Keiko who died only one year ago. Like so many of her friends now gone, she thinks, I'm almost the last. Only three years before there was Keiko at the Skeena reunion. And then after this summer by the Skeena River, she will spend her life back in Don Mills at the home of her daughter, her son-in-law and her daughter.

Those days she lived with her sister. The 300-block flat on Powell in Little Tokyo, Vancouver days. They would be shopping — so excited, a vase for the table at Woodward's on Hastings, two cup and saucers. She recalls bone china, ones from England for tea time, the soda crackers with butter and jam, toasted — the two of them, would just be Kane and her, through the revolving doors at Woodward's, then back home, their little flat on the 300-block.

Or then those days living with Kishimotos on Fulton Street, alone, over Kishimoto's store, it was Prince Rupert, her father fishing near the Queen Charlotte Islands. She would be there, at the front window, up the street from Cow Bay, they would go to eat Chinese food at West End when he came in from fishing, and she would be at the front window, watching all the boats rushing back to the canneries of Cow Bay.

And the black and orange oil tanker is motionless, from where now she is standing, sixty years ago, still breath held in her body.

She recalls the way it was then as now, her heart to Gloria, to Toronto and the present, her future, house on Plateau Crescent, Don Mills, the carport, the rhodendrons lush and pink in the garden of the neighbours. Thinks of the bazaar at the Japanese Canadian Cultural Centre, all the hakkujin who now come to eat teriyaki and sushi at the Centre, it was Raymond Moriyama, his design, thinks of Plateau, Gloria's kind hakkujin neighbours. And she shifts the

receiver with her ear, hangs it there squeezed, here in a space, voices
jammed with such present, how it fills the ear, distant tense bridge,
and veil mists hang to cusp of time, that vocabulary is bone in ear,
cheek, shoulder and sad hip. ('Kane, Kane, be here,' she thinks, and
thinks about her mother.')

And so push at the inner corners of her eyes, upper lip which
delicately holds, weighing once more, melody this, her daughter is,
child, is an infant, a baby held to her breast, it is still then,
'Ma-uh-uh, Mama,' Gloria's young voice, little girl to hold, voice
faltering and trembling back into the throat, Gloria, she'd wet her
pants in class, 'Mama... mama...'

And then, it is her voice on the phone, when Michiko answers
to the ringing, from Toronto.

('Shimpai shinai no yo. Nan-de-mo-nai,' it was then, 'Don't worry,'
Michiko reassured.)

Gloria, Gloria's voice, outwards.

(She looks towards her daughter, now it is some years later, Gloria
at age thirteen, because it was when they moved to Henry Street,
Gloria already taller than her mother, and it is the kitchen. The
African violets Michiko has just bought from Eaton's College Street.
'Nan-deh-moh-nai,' those words repeated on what occasions
through the years and of that afternoon after school when her
daughter was only eight.

She had washed the soiled pants with Cheer detergent, the
voice of a daughter, she'd felt the pull, narrowing in her eyes, twinge

at the wrists, upper lip delicately forming the silence. Washing, then flattening through the rollers of a machine bought on credit, one dollar a week, each week the salesman's face at the door.)

This witness it is, this thing of family, the walls of home press on the ears, to attend, memory in the turning wrist, the soup-dashi, quickly, precisely sieved, a distant bridge, to join day to day the smell, Shogatsu to Shogatsu, all the years, family gathering, mochi and baked lucky redfish, parsley, shiso leaf fragrant, and vanishes before the cooking hands, of labour, of wear, into the kitchen air.

('Gloria,' she says, 'do you remember? That story I told you before about grandfather? We used to have African violets on Powell Street. He always dressed with neat pressed starched shirts. He would shave himself with the straight razor as he stood in front of the mirror, so clean, he would look at me in the corner of the mirror. I think at these times he was thinking about me without my mama.

'And he was always neat. Ne? The smell of the shaving cream and the talcum is what I remember. Ne? Elastic armbands, striped shirt, the stiff collar — this is what I told you about. Even back then, you see, he said, "You must speak Japanese, but it's more important to speak perfect English. I want you to go to school." This is the kind of person he was. He always had a fountain pen clasped neatly to his shirt breast-pocket. Ne, Gloria.

'He used to cut my hair with such a razor, at home in the kitchen, I'd feel, you know. The hair feels like it's a brush on the back of your neck when the hair is cut short, very short?

'Ahh. And one day, he was at White Lunch on Hastings Street, it was in Vancouver. A waitress and another laughed at him because he made some mistake with his English, they thought it was funny. But most of the time the waitresses were very nice to us. But this one, and he just said in a clear voice that he was Naturalized, a fisherman, and union secretary. I was proud of his accent just then as he told me.' And when Gloria asks, does Michiko recall clearly enough if she was there too at White Lunch, the anger pent up, the booth, where was it they were sitting, or was it just her father who told her?

'Anyways...')

But then when he would come in drunk some nights, she reminds herself. He would tell her to go into the other room. This time she was living with him, just after her father took her from schoolgirl, just for the summer months. She would put her face in the pillow, bury it there, pillow tightly against her ears.

She heard him. And she heard him singing Japanese songs. Saké. It was already late. Japanese singing. Ton-ton-ton. Saké, saké toh. It was on the Fraser River. Ton-ton-ton. His voice was good, though just sometimes it would go off-key, the crooning, with the drink in his glass, as he beat the table, the Japanese fishing rhythms. Ton-ton-ton.

'He was called Jimmy by the hakkujin. Jimmy. Fishermen like to drink when they come home. But it was "nigi-yakka."'

Another story she tells one day to Gloria is about the time her father had taken her up to live on the northcoast. It is why she ended up at Kishimoto's, alone, Kane, her older sister still in Vancouver. Every once in a while she will tell Gloria this story. The time steering towards the Queen Charlotte Islands, when they sailed into storm.

'I'll always remember this, Gloria. Do you know what he told me before we left?

'"Since your mother died, that was sad, especially for you and your sister. You've just been working so hard as schoolgirl at Mrs. McDougall's." This was the place on Nicola Street. He was in Steveston at Atlas Cannery.

'He said to me, "They are a good family, but I didn't want this to happen to you, I couldn't do anything else. But you know, Mich, one evening, I think, I was, this was when I was working near Tofino on Vancouver Island. And it was quiet on the beach, there was no rain, it had just stopped. It was so bright. I was humming Soran-bushi and I could see you much happier. You would be playing piano in a big hall in the east, maybe Montreal, maybe Toronto."

'And I was so happy with him, happy even though I just then thought of my harmonica, my mother. I looked at him and it was like that look in the shaving mirror. The air smelled so clean with salt, I had a bit of green string, fishing cord in my hands. His eyes strained, you know, between the eyes, like when he was angry, but it was something else, my mother. He caught my look.

'"What is it, Michiko? Why do you look at me with that kind of eye?" And then he grinned.

'"But anyway, you've learned to become a woman. I'm surprised, because not just your older sister Kane, but even you. Now I think you must be at school, just school. You are still a young girl. You must be a young girl."

'So this was his wish and it was mine too, ne.

'And that night when he'd just finished saying this, we stood there looking up the coast and I was dreaming of Alaska. I knew

Queen Charlotte Islands were near there. One New Year's a friend of my father's was talking about halibut fishing, big halibut up there.

'Then I asked him. "Have you seen Alaska before, father?" and he nodded just once. His head, his chin held up, the smooth skin of his chin. I remember always the sweet smell of spice after shave lotion. "My English is not good enough, but yours will be perfect. This is the way for Nihonjin in Canada."'

And there she was beside him on deck, the two of them moving into the night before them. Her mouth wet, comforted, the music of her harmonica filled the air.

And the night black sky had become more white, these storm clouds, their heavy rains, and it had come suddenly and the boat, a twenty-five footer, engulfed. Her father had told Michiko to go into the small cabin, told her to just lie down, not move. She buried her face in the pillow like the times when he had been drunk. But the boat was out of control, tossed back and forth, rolled onto the rocks, she could hear the grinding hull. There was no light. She fell from the bed, was rolled back and forth on the floor. She did not once open her eyes. And she knew her father could not come as she wept. Her face crashed against wood, jostled there, could not think, felt the impact of the pounding. An enamel kettle fell, then the rolling on the floor just beyond her.

Somehow it had passed, or felt like it. Her father had finally opened the door.

'"You okay, Mich?" just this, but his tone was embracing and kind. "We are okay now." He had been so quiet afterwards for a while, just kept holding onto her hand.

'We were towed by a hakkujin fisherman into China Hut. Water had gone into the engine through a hole. I learned this after. I mostly see my father's face, his control, when he opened the door.

And then we were being towed, Ocean Prince was the name of his boat. I always think of that name when there's something about Prince Charles. Funny, ne?'

'Then, mother, you went to Swanson Bay, wasn't it?' Gloria says.

'We were towed into Prince Rupert from there. Then my father sent me back to Swanson Bay. I stayed there. Myself, because Papa was going on.'

'Yes, mother. And you stayed in Swanson Bay for a few months, I remember.'

'At first it was hard, ne Gloria. But I stayed with a kind lady. Then, somebody asked, "Do you want to go live in Prince Rupert or back to Vancouver?" Of course, ne, Vancouver. But my father sent word. I was to be sent to Rupert and my heart was broken. All my classmates at the dock, coming there, saying "goodbye, Michi."

'And then, do you know, Gloria, that night only Kishimoto san at the dock to meet me. I cried so much, alone in bed, and only after I prayed to Kami-sama, was I able to sleep.'

'That's why you never made it to Queen Charlotte Islands, ne, mom?' Gloria's tone as if this is a new realization, though she's heard the story many times. 'But grandfather, that's when he went to Sandspit, ne?'

'So this is the time I go to Borden Street School in Rupert.'

When she had been young, much younger than now her daughter is, she'd become sad, walking with her older sister in Vancouver. 'Kane, today I'm going to sign up for the play at the Japanese Hall.' Walking with her sister from Strathcona Public School, up Gore Avenue to Powell Street across from Powell Ground, home of baseball; and then she'd go to do the grocery shopping, cook dinner, do laundry, sad with her hip and leg, the way you carry, not a physical pain, but still the body, carry a thing, loss. She carried this thing they both held onto, walked almost in step together, rhythm, hand in hand, her older sister there. And then even, not there.

And how it was Prince Rupert that changed things, there alone even without Kane, and without her mother. Rupert. The Kishimotos were kind, but she would sit there looking from Borden Street School, where now, on this last visit in her seventies, now a children's playground is there. Rupert, she would dream — right into Cow Bay. Prince Rupert and how you grow up, you're still quite young. 'You're still young, Michi,' she hears Kishimoto-san's, Oi-san's thin clear voice. Oi-san. It is, at this time, sockeye season on the Skeena.

But now to think of such things, as also the times it's been repeated to others, and she listens herself, she thinks, 'Ara! These stories feel like some thing away, funny, uh?' That she no longer knows the exact feelings, but those which give heat, the moment when she says them, words, voices in her, and then she begins, says it to Gloria — or to her two sons, Kevin and Roy. And then it does come back and she gets a feeling, it's lonely but warm. It feels like singing, a bit, she thinks. Her palms are closed, and she feels that she holds a warmth, something like a fever, the dry lines in her skin.

And it was the same almost when the Sansei student, Kiyo, had come to talk to her once, though more about her time in Port Essington during the evacuation time, but she started talking about her girlhood, too, just a little. Kiyo, from the University of Alberta.

Lethbridge. She had known the young student's uncle back in Victoria, Kadowaki-san.

Only once did she mention it to Gloria. 'You know, when you are young, you think you'll always think about your parents. But it's been a long time, so much you know. You forget things. The past. It's like that, especially about my mother. But, maybe I think about when I was young more often. Some things I remember. But then I forget. And I used to go to cemetery for my father's grave. Father's Day. But then we always used to go on Father's Day. But now sometimes, it gets late a little. A couple of days. Just to put some flowers there. The bushes get overgrown, a little.' And as she sniffed at the soup dashi fumes, she thought of talking about this again, but then didn't want to bother Gloria about these thoughts.

'Thanks, last time Mama, for supper,' said Gloria.

'Oh, I felt so badly, you and Bobby came all the way from Kitchener, from Oi-san to Obasan's. Such a long way, and I forgot to buy sukiyaki meat. Day before, I was at church. There was a meeting for the bazaar. Day you came, that morning I was thinking for a long time, so.'

'It was okay, great, Mother,' Gloria said.

'Really?' she asked. 'I used frozen sirloin tip from the freezer. It was okay? No. And I wanted to make a nice clear soup. Next time, phone sooner. You phoned that morning. I want to make a good meal for Bob. Bobby enjoys eating so much. There wasn't enough last time.'

'Mother. It doesn't matter, ne?' Gloria's voice, a faint turn of impatience.

Michiko is small, four feet and eight inches when she was

younger, now even shorter, her back slightly hunched. She doesn't always wear the skirts and shifts she once did. Often, it's slacks, lightweight — even in winter — though darker doubleknits in winter, as now, which Gloria buys for her at Simpson's. She still has one new pair in the Simpson's bag, like that for four months now. She took to slacks about ten years ago, and easily, though her youngest son Kevin had said, 'It's weird seeing you in pants, mom. But it's okay I guess. Ya.'

She waters her African violets by the window in the living room. Such flowers she's transported to every place she's lived ever since she first bought them at Eaton's. Transplanted, repotted and repotted them, so many of them now, and she's given so many away.

It was odd for her at first. She was so used to having her violets in the kitchen, ever since days in BC. In their first home, a flat over a fur shop in the Jewish section of downtown Toronto, she had over two dozen on a metal table by the fridge. It was one of those utility tables with two tiers which everyone seemed to have. She'd also neatly piled her Loblaw's Supermarket Lucky Green Stamp Books there, on the second tier.

When they moved to the house on Henry Street six years later, she had first thought she could not get used to a house without windows in the kitchen. But she had, after a few months (she remembered how every morning the first few weeks her heart had sunk when she'd come out to the kitchen to make coffee and had to switch on the lights. But her children had come in to make it bright with its pale pale blue wallpaper with yellow flowers, subtle, not too strong). And the new white melamine cupboards with modern brushed chrome handles are so easy, clean, and do not seem to get so soiled and gray about the handles. It seems she hardly has to wipe them.

The dashi is just about right now, it mustn't boil, the kombu nor the katsuo— the dried fish flakes— just to the point of boiling; then it is filtered clear. The room is soft, radiant around the ceiling light, and it gently sparkles as she handles the sieve in her hand, for there's a bare humid haze. Yet, it is morning still and bright in the front room by the pots of African violets.

When the phone rings, she tries to hurry, her foot swollen, into the dining room with its diffused light, its half-opened tassled blinds. Sometimes difficult to tell in this house whether it is evening or daytime. She catches the phone on the seventh ring.

She breathes out hard, a small straight gasp.

'Hello? Oh, Gloria, I was running.' She answers, 'Yes, okay-yo. Yes, okay-yo.'

She looks towards the front room bay window, violets among several other plants on a long white table, plastic sheeting protecting from any spill, the hardwood floor below.

'Today? Okay.' And then she listens. 'Maybe tempura would be good, ne? I'll look in the freezer, see if I have nice big shrimps. Maybe udon. What would you like?'

'Soh... soh...' she breathes out as her daughter's voice takes on a tone of concern and thoughtful probing, decision.

'He's been sleeping all morning,' Michiko explains. 'He ate a little last night.' It is then Gloria who speaks for minutes without stop, still feeling her way through. And there is now in Michiko's kitchen the smell of baked salted dog salmon cooling on the kitchen table. And there is the fresh scent of cucumbers, so thinly sliced, a gentle hand with salt and rice vinegar, the draw of moisture.

'Gloria. I think this way is best. At home, he prefers I think, I don't know, ne? Shimpai-keh-doh-ne?

'Oh, I know, sometimes. He doesn't know, but sometimes I get like that too, I forget, I feel pressure in my head. You know. Can't do anything when you get old... I lose my balance. Ne. You know...

'So... so... that's true, ne. Maybe later. The hospital, maybe later, I think, ne. Yesterday he wanted something to drink, whiskey — Johnnie Walker. Ya, just like before... Anyways...'

And then he said, he held up his hands, shaped them like fish mouths, said they were — salmon, sockeye, they were there, up in front of him, coming up to eat. He was on the boat.

'Have you eaten mazze-gohan lately? What did Bobby's mama make for you Sunday? She's a good cook.'

Out in the front room, through the white sheers comes the bright sun of mid-morning, November, a weekday, and quiet, morning-tea quiet.

Out in the front room is the bright sun of mid-morning, a weekday in November, and quiet, morning-tea quiet.

This front room, almost a perfect fifteen-foot square, is filled with this bright, the sun's direct rays fall diagonally right to left across a burgundy floral-print sofa along the wall to the left-hand side of the window from her view. A glass-topped coffee table is opposite the sofa. Opposite this is a matching chair, with a matching end table near the room's front. The violets are in the bay window amidst other green plants on a long white table; below, the floor is hardwood and covered by a plastic dropsheet in case of spills. A radio is on FM, music is not too strong, plays comfortably in the background. Now the news is almost over, 'Weather is next' says the voice, before a commercial chimes in.

And there has been a sudden drop in temperature over the last two days, and following a week-long stretch of flat gray days, it is now bright, sunny, and the front room gets warm with the heat of afternoon light and the furnace now turned to winter degrees. Soon, in the evenings, she will stand sometimes with her back to the heat vent, arms tucked behind her, her sweater, a cream cardigan with neat pearl buttons all the way up.

Through the white sheers is the sun's morning bright. But also, both furiously and gently, a sky filled with thick wet flakes of snow.

And in the snow flurry is Gloria, walking up the driveway. In one hand she is carrying her car keys, in the other, her right, a parcel. From across the street there comes the smell of smoke from a nearby chimney, the frigid sunny blue.

In the two local dailies, the Thursday editions had articles on winter getaway holiday destinations, Cancun, the Dominican, Freeport and the like. The fashion pages, meanwhile, showed the current year's vacation cruisewear, the theme being Canadian designers.

Gloria is careful with her load, for she is delivering this parcel to Michiko. She is returning from the cemetery, the crematorium office. It is exactly fifteen days after the death of her father. Sticking up and out from her shoulder bag, half-unzipped, can be seen a booklet-brochure for vacations. It is of the Bahamas. Her mother hasn't been on a real vacation somewhere, elsewhere, for over thirty years.

Gloria can't help thinking back, as to why she, they, couldn't stop laughing — barely holding in the laughter when she and her brothers first went to the funeral parlour to discuss arrangements for the otsuya, service and the rest. It happens.

I know a friend, she was once close, who spent months tending her dying father. He was dying slowly though comparatively peacefully with a degenerative heart ailment. Some people would say that she and her mother were having a fairly easy time of it. He was neither suffering horrendously, nor was the death sudden when it did come, acute with the anguish of horror, pain and things left unuttered, unexpressed, the regret of wanting another chance.

It took me by surprise when they told me that they were taking turns going on a week-long vacation to the Caribbean 'during' his hospitalization. But then his condition, the doctors assured them, would be stable for at least six weeks, and he'd been terminal and attended to with care for over a year. I'd seen the wear on the mother's face though her daughter, my close friend (we'd grown up together) seemed cheery as ever, I knew her well, her every mood and expression.

After she told me about the situation, we'd met for a drink 'far from the hospital, Gerry,' at her request. I naturally agreed. Some friends, even a cousin of hers, still couldn't get it, agree with their 'escapes.' 'We told him... and you know, Ger, I still see his smile on his face, the way he waved his hand, okay. Come back with a tan.'

The feelings around illness and dying of those we know are like that. Death can be sudden or not, and horrendous with suffering, or rather calm; and with it come the questions and judgements, of self, from self, of others and from others, such closet of clutter.

I've been for quite some time concerned here. I have been wondering why and how Michiko seemed rather arbitrarily in Prince Rupert, talking on the phone. It seemed natural enough. Yet, it did not, it eventually became clear that it seemed such an unlikely situation. But she was just there. So I shifted, crossed intentions out and in, seeking a natural flow: Michiko there in Rupert. The black and orange oil tanker. The sense it makes, or seems to make, how we poke and try.

Yet, I realize something. How the last time and the other times I myself have been there, in Rupert, I really wanted my own Mum there, thought of her up there on the upper part of town overlooking Cow Bay on Borden Street, where she went to Borden Street Public School, and now she would have seen the kid's playground with swings. I took a photograph of that spot, she was in my mind's eye. Yet at her age and her health it's not something I can realistically imagine happening. It's just that way, unfortunately. It would be wonderful, though.

And so, what follows are some facts I feel compelled to add, a homage of sorts:

My mother's name is Mitsuko (née Mukai) Shikatani. She was born in Inverness Cannery, near Prince Rupert, BC, in 1908 (there's nothing there now except for a government sign, marking the place, the Skeena River and bush. Last summer my oldest brother and I just stood there together looking — a few fishing boats, their nets out and drifting). My mother lived in British Columbia in Steveston, in Vancouver (her most cherished moments of her life, she tells me, was for two years at the age of seventeen with her older sister; she acted and sang in local Nikkei stage productions). Then she went to Prince Rupert, then Port Essington, and during the war years, she (and my family) were in Slocan. Ever since, she has lived in Toronto.

As I am writing this, snow is falling outside. I see this through the kitchen window. It is February, a day before my birthday on the 6th, and it's a cold snap we're in, about minus 15 Celsius. In the spring — in Montreal that very possibly might not be until late April — I'll pick some Saturday, get up early and strip off the plastic sheeting taped up to keep the cold out. But for now, as I look up, my face is warm. And it's bathed beautifully in the direct path of sunlight.

B

The weather in Paris lately has been strange, rather unpredictable. They say it's like that all over — it's even strange back home in North America. Quite a heatwave, I read, I read it in The Herald Tribune. They, the news, TV and radio, talk about it, they suggest it's partly the greenhouse effect — the thinning of the ozone layer everybody worries about these days. And I guess they're right. I can't ignore it any more than anyone else.

But my thoughts, I admit, aren't really there. Paris, I know, is very hot, oppressive. It's horrible, this city, the humidity. The hot thick stink of the Métro, the blast of furnace hits you when you descend underground. I sweat all day, it pours off me. I'm burning up, sometimes so flushed I can feel the fever in my face. Around me the faces of others, at far less distress.

I recall a winter I spent here a few years back, the first year I'd moved to Europe from Canada. I prayed for weather like this. Untrue. I don't pray. Religion has never been much in my life. As the last in a family of nine siblings, a lot of such things of rearing fell by the way.

My parents had gradually lost interest in bringing up the last three offspring in any religious way. Not to say I was religionless at home — my parents were Anglican. But as Japanese Canadians, there was always this otherness, some Buddha, some Shinto-type feeling in our home. My grandfather, who lived with us, was Buddhist. Kami, the Japanese word for gods, for instance, I know because my folks occasionally spoke of Kami-sama and my mother would place bits of food in front of a household altar, especially at New Year's — which stood on the mantle in the front room, that altar where now I think of my grandparents. 'For risen spirits of the deceased,' I was told. Spirits which would also have flared as fire when they died.

Oh, this heat is really awful. I can't seem to take it. It's weird it's so hot, without any change.

That winter a few years back was also very odd. I was living near Montparnasse on the rue Delambre. Hotel de Deux Balcons was the name which was written in neon in turquoise (the 'x' however was broken) just outside the window of my room. But the hotel, when I registered the first day, was apparently called Au Bon Sommeil.

'Y'a pas encore de balcons, voyez,' Madame Passard, the proprietor, had told me. The balconies, she'd never even seen them since the time she and her husband Jean-Louis Voultier had owned the place — about the time of the student riots in '68. I made some joke about how it was heaven, a hotel of God, you know, Dieu, like deux. They didn't seem to get it, though they were pleasant enough.

It was a terrible winter. I read in the papers that it was the worst winter in Europe in decades. It had snowed so much in Paris that for four straight days the buses stopped moving. The military was brought in, trucked commuters in from the suburbs and back. The palms and olive trees in Nice, the Promenade des Anglais, had suffered, the journalists had reported 'irreparable damage.'

'Such snow, like in your country, monsieur,' Madame said to me one day when we'd met by chance at the corner café, Le Galion.

'I guess this is no big potatoes to you, this cold,' Thierry the barman had also humoured. Potatoes? I wondered.

Can I imagine such a winter, such cold as I lie here now? Funny. I froze that winter, swore how much I thrived in the heat, and now here, listen. I run drearily, so drearily on, about the weather, so — I don't know. Maybe in some way trying to distract my thoughts, deflect them. This thickness, a heavy weight that's been in my chest for weeks now, won't go away. It's had me a bit worried.

I think about this short breath. Right now, I can't inhale much, so short, especially as I lie on my back. Doesn't feel as if I'm taking in enough air. Sweat, too, I've been sweating in this small stuffy room. A cold sweat, different — I worry about that — as I've often stared like this towards the gray white of a muggy sky, the small square of a window which looks six flights down to the rue Fosse Geoffroy.

This, the discomfort of my nights in the past month. Each night feeling that I'll stop breathing if I fall asleep. Somehow, eventually I drift off — of course — and sometimes it's okay. But often, in the middle of the night I wake, perhaps only for a few seconds, very intense with anxiety, a burning around my head, my thighs, perspiration. I kick off the thin cotton sheet and then. And then, well, I don't know, I am somehow asleep again, sleep easily until morning.

I awake well rested, as I am now, lying here. But when I open my eyes, I don't move, can't seem to. Just lie there for a while, listen to the traffic, hear the science students on their way to the Jussieu Faculty of the Sorbonne. About me are the dismal soiled colours — a peachy rose tone and dark yellow in this tiny rectangular space, a space where from my poor mattress I count the cobwebs in the high corners, the strings of dust waving like hair in the dull light, imagine the silverfish slithering sudden by the basin and bidet.

I shouldn't complain about this place. It's true that in Paris any room so close to the Sorbonne, Pantheon and such is a find. It is after all temporary. I'm still looking for a permanent home and this really is not so bad. Though maybe I'm more the Bastille trendy type. It's interim and I'm fortunate. When my friend Marie-Pierre told me about it — it belongs to her parents — they're Jewish — French Jews, why I mention this I'm not sure. And Marie-Pierre called me one day, 'Kevin, my parents have this little space — it was a chambre de bonne — you can have it if it's temporary.' (How long has it been now?) 'If it's temporary,' she said, 'as long as you don't talk much to the gardien.' I agreed, naturally. Didn't question about the gardien. Not my business. And so I asked, 'How much, Marie-Pierre?'

She just shrugged, ignored my words. And then a little later she said, '47 francs.'

And when I got here I said to her, 'It's all right, just fine,' and it was she who pointed out the dust. It had rested unoccupied for over a year. Apparently a cousin from Philadelphia had last been. 'While on some training period,' said Marie-Pierre.

First thing after Marie-Pierre left me to my privacy ('Dinner, not this week but next, that's agreeable, Kevin?'), I took an old broom which was jamming closed a small door. It was in a cupboard by the corner kitchenette. (There's one of those primitive affairs fitted for those large bright blue tanks of Camping-Gaz, and I'm having most of my meals at the couscous-and-frites joint down the street). I tried to sweep but all I did was scratch up clouds of aggravating dust from the soiled orange broadloom, with me and my allergies. The stuff just hung there in the dormant stale air. I didn't open the door much because I'd seen a cockroach scurrying out of the corridor light outside #5, diagonally across from my room. This dust caught in my throat immediately and in my lungs. My forearms became prickly.

Nothing has improved to any extent, the dust, nor the smell, even with the window thrown open every day and there's the chirping of sparrows (I guess they are) who home in the nearby Jardin des Plantes. I stopped any major cleaning, have put back the broom against the door. The cobwebs, strings of feathery dust remain caught as I stare upward from my bed.

I've grown used to it now, the dusty threads, taken ownership of the room and its dirt — and so, it is mine, and somehow it is not so disgusting, and it is there today in the morning beams of light entering the room. The particles are fine, a mist, a thin layer of heat, fever, the sweat in bed, this August morning.

I close my eyes, there is music, a thrumming, not the sounds of students. There are the sparrows; but also a singing I recognize which returns me to Canada. It is not the urban southeast, my home, but the Pacific northwest which calls, a reprise to a single time, a couple of days in my life. The music is bird-like, and it is leather-like, evokes the damp moist perfume of cedar, alder, and salmon and sawmill on the water. It's a memory of fishermen and canneries — of Japanese, Chinese, Indian nations, Finnish and Norwegians — living with the mountains and river tides of my family's first home in America, the Skeena, Skeena River.

My eyes open once more. I see a bracelet. Moving in a slow wavering circle about the room, the colours — turquoise, scarlet and pale yellow — shimmering, caught in the window light, mid-air. It is like the feathery dust. I shut my eyes, not firmly. The hard weight, pressure.

The singing now has left my ears. The sound of a bus, the #87 headed for Place d'Italie, coming to a stop, barely up the block, adds now to the pitch of the birds. When I open my eyes, the wavering movement remains, the low tracing of a circle in the morning light above the quotidian street.

My breath is heavy still, but for a moment runs startlingly clear. I wonder, as I stare at this moving object of light, why such a thing stays with you when you know it is not real, that by simply rising from bed, brushing teeth, spitting out the gummy foul of night and thus descending to the pedestrian circuit, all — all will be eliminated without further complication.

It happened five years ago. B came up to me, introduced herself. A teenaged girl — like any you'd see in a small northern Canadian town. I was in Prince Rupert to do some research on the new North Pacific Cannery Museum for a friend who was making a film about the history of Japanese-Canadian fishing in BC. My parents and older sisters had lived in the area before the last war. Sent into the BC interior like the rest of the Japanese Canadians, they had returned to the Skeena River briefly at Sunnyside Cannery in the '50s. Since my childhood it had been a romantic otherworld, place of mystery and legend, of spoken history.

When the local library heard of my visit, they asked me to speak on my interests there and my family's experiences. It had gone well. I felt a celebrity among local history buffs. My parents' home, Port Essington, no longer existed, but in Rupert now the name held magic, was a legendary ghost of the Skeena. Once it had been called Spokeshute, its Indian name. I'd never been to Rupert before, but the people, more than the landscape, gave me a strong sense of self, stronger than I'd felt in years.

'Welcome home,' one guy, a young teenager sitting near the back had called out. He was Indian, and I felt elated as he smiled.

Even now, I am held by that night, and I remember B when I first noticed her. I remember her.

She came up to me in the corridor just after I'd retrieved my coat. I was heading to have a drink at a bar with a small group from the historical society.

'I know what you mean,' she said, blurted softly, edgy rehearsed words. But she relaxed immediately when we traded grins. She bit her bottom lip.

'I really related to that stuff you were saying about your roots and all.'

I recall her clearly, I have ever since. She was a regular teenager. Neatly groomed, scrubbed, you might say. Dark brown hair, blunt cut to the chin — a boyish way, thin dark eyebrows, probably drawn more intensely. Her eyes, beautiful, and a bit of lipstick. Over slim blue jeans she wore a button-down collar shirt. Pink and white nylon joggers. Her fingernails might have had polish on.

The thing about her name was odd, fun.

'Your name's Beatrice? The B's for Beatrice?'

'B,' she replied. 'Just "B,"' she explained.

'Just B? The letter?'

'Yup, just the letter.'

I was briefly silent.

'I should explain. It's what you said about the smell here? Like you said the smell of salmon, fish in the air because of the canneries? The boats docked up, you know? You said the smell was familiar and all that? That even though you weren't from the Skeena, your family was from Port Essington and somebody had sent you fish back east? So I'm, at least my dad was. He was fisherman like your dad, and my grandad and his father, too.'

'In Essington, yeah?'

'Uh-huh. I grew up in Terrace, but we've lived all along the Skeena, on the Naas River, too.' Her fingers pulled down at her sleeve which was long, to cover her hand the way teenaged girls sometimes do. She was sweet and I was thrilled to be speaking, to be having a good conversation, a nice one, with a cute teenager at that.

'I'm Finnish, eh? Or part, you know...'

She was then silent.

She had, it seemed, a charm — and she stood there, her eyes slightly downcast. I wanted to say something to engage her more, but what else was there to say? For a half-minute we just stood there. I was self-conscious, ready to excuse myself.

'You know, you should try to get to Essington,' B then softly blurted out.

It would be wonderful, I thought. It had become, I gathered, a real ghost town. Some pilings and a few buildings barely standing. A couple of Indians and a few old Finns left from that fishing community were still about, I had heard.

'Not really,' B said. 'But it's neat out there — kind of spooky. People who aren't used to it think it all looks pretty eerie out on the Skeena. My uncle took me to Essington once. It's beautiful, amazing when there's sun on the Skeena.'

I asked B: 'Hey, I've got to meet some people for a drink. Why don't you come?'

'Nah. No thanks, anyway. I don't think I'm,' she giggled slightly. 'Besides, I'm not old enough to get in, unless you have ID for me.'

I smiled and before I could say any more, she turned. 'Well, see y'around, eh?' She raised her right arm, barely a couple of inches in a kind of quick abrupt wave, still clutching her long sleeve with her hand.

That is how the Skeena came to grip me. An evening I still think about — for I can see it, hear it, as I lie here.

After all the beer and good talk, I'd gone back to the hotel so exhilarated, did not care about the rain pouring down, the constant rain of that northern BC coast, Rupert nights, Kaien Island nights, as I paid for a self-serve coffee at the Chevron, convenience store open all night, across the street from my route home, and then pulled off my socks, my damp cotton trousers, switched on the TV of my hotel room, stretched out on my bed in my shorts, hair wet, my feet still cold, clammy. I thought then of my brief taste of celebrity and the kind people, of the three days left for me there, felt so sad, and thought especially of B. But that was that, I said to myself, that was that, that was that.

Two mornings later I was walking along Third Avenue headed towards the town archives at the municipal buildings. I entered a restaurant, Double Happiness it was called, one of several places for both Canadian and Chinese food in Rupert, and there weren't any Chinese characters on the window or the sign. Double Happiness, and it was a dismal place, with dark beige booths and empty Chinese lanterns among the overhead fluorescent lights.

I heard a voice.

I looked up from my coffee. It was B.

She stood there briefly, we chatted. She was working, here, part time.

'You're still here, eh?' she said. It was actually the second time she'd said that, but it was shy and eventful, wanting-to-talk type talk. And that's how it began, the second experience with B, why she is still with me in my mind as I lie here, listening now to birds from the Jardin des Plantes, watching the dust streamers catch my wheezy breath as a breeze passes over my legs to my sweaty crotch beneath my briefs, the sound of the #87, another one coming to its air-brake stop. It then pulls away for Place d'Italie.

She'd gone once to Port Essington along the Skeena. She just said Essington, the way people there just say Rupert or Port Ed for Port Edward. It had been with her uncle, she said, said again, and I said, 'Uh-huh, I remember you telling me that the other night,' and she said, realizing, 'Oh, yeah,' and then I eventually blurted, 'Isn't it a real coincidence, meeting you again? Actually, I'd hoped I would... it was just real great talking to you before,' and she said, 'Not a big town.'

'Yeah, it's really neat, I was telling my boyfriend Steve about talking to you. I'll remember you, Mr. Yoshida.'

'Kevin.' I smiled, and I agreed. 'You know, when I travel around — I do quite a bit with my work and all. Well, it's a pretty small world. I really like coincidences.'

'Well, if you haven't been to Essington, you wanna go? Steve's got his boat tied down at Tyee, just across from Essington. C'mon, whatcha think?' She pulled her mouth down on one side.

Steve was part Tsimshian, part Norwegian.

'It's safe? I hear it's pretty rough on the Skeena out there?'

'No problem,' she said. 'The boat's a skiff, you know, a big flat-bottom? About twenty feet. The motor's really powerful.'

'All right!' she said when I agreed, it was with soft exclamation and instantly I felt her silken young wit.

I was eating Alaska black cod hours later, back at the Double Happiness. Black cod — my cousin had brought it back east with him after each fishing season in Skeena. It connected me to this place. Double Happiness, the tart lemon, the smoky velvet of alder in the watery juices from steam cooking, I was anxious. B and Steve were to pick me up in twenty minutes.

Steve, I'd meet him, Steve who fished the herring since a kid, out of Port Ed. And as I listened to the radio, the local announcer sounding no different from elsewhere, the music a familiar yet unrecognizable pop tune, a picture of my dead father came to mind, of him in Essington, the River of Mists called Skeena, I thought of sweet B and her friend Steve. Soon I would be on the river which carried family history, yet unknown. Melancholy as much as excitement filled me. Double Happiness, I said quietly to myself. And just then, my father and his bond to the Skeena were present, entered my body.

Summer days are long on the Skeena, it's that far north up the British Columbia coast. Much further and one is in the Alaska Panhandle.

'What I like here is how there's so much daylight, the day just goes on and on,' I said to the two in front of me, in the front seat of the beat-up Tracer I was a passenger in.

It was not yet the height of midsummer. But nevertheless the daylight would stretch to 11 p.m., the night. And the sun rose early at this time. It was a place and time when one would sleep while the sun, already beaming at the blinds at 3 a.m., would outline the window's shape with a perimetric pencil of white light.

'Get used to it,' Steve answered. 'But yeah, you're right, guess it's all right, pretty good. I don't know what it's like any other way. 'Cept once I went down to Vancouver.'

Steve was tall, with straight darkish blond hair, which was long and over the neck of the Oakland Raiders jersey he wore. He had not said much up to then and would not say much more for the rest of the drive. When B had introduced him, she'd grabbed him by the shirtsleeve, literally pulled him over to me, my own eyes had gone straight into his, they were so lightning blue, he was boyish cute more than handsome, though his face, up close, was scarred, an old cut on his forehead and the creases and pocks of teenage blemishes. He kind of rocked forward upon his boot-cut joggers, hunched over, gave me a quick agreeable two-twitch nod, barely said 'Hi,' though his grin was straight, uncomplicated.

They looked sweet together, and now they sat close as their seatbelts would allow them as we zipped down the two-lane road, a thin mist falling, the wipers going. More than anything, I had been stunned by the presence of the low white ghost-like clouds, some thick, heavy, others like long snaking threads, hanging and spun into the black mountains and towering islands. The water of the Skeena, muddy brown in spots, dark green in others, is the water home of salmon which go upstream to spawn. The salmon, delicious, the taste of dense sweet oil, fat belly of fish, smoked as well, and watching this river, though this was far from taste, the feelings which seemed to float in my mouth as I watched the river through the windows, seemed to hold me by throat and lungs to the tides, the salt water and glaciers which together formed the power of the Skeena.

'Neat huh, Kevin? We're going up to Essington, both of us. We're both kids of fishermen from there? You're from the east, from the city, and I guess you're, you're quite a bit older than me, huh?' She looked back to me. Steve took a quick glance at B, grinned as he turned his gaze back onto the road up ahead.

'See the eagle up there, Kevin?' he asked me. 'Ever seen one of those before? You don't see those back east, eh? It's a bald eagle. I used to come out just round Essington with my grandfather, eh? We'd just watch. And he'd tell me stories about when he fished with his grandfather.'

I began again, 'This is an amazing trip, I don't believe it, just.' And through the mist, I saw the eagle appearing then disappearing, high above the river. It seemed that I was at a brink of entry, at the tone of Steve's voice, what he, without drama, spoke of. I wanted to probe further with Steve, but yet knew to hold back. I did not want to spoil this, felt my own silence in a way I'd never before. The eagle now gone, a glacial peak briefly dazzled with sun through the mist.

B spoke. 'God, I'm getting really excited? Essington — that's going to be ama...zing. I'm glad you're here.' She looked towards me.

I grinned. And she said: 'It's like this, coming to Rupert. And you'll take some of the old Skeena back with you. But you know, you'll also leave part of yourself here in the Skeena, eh?' Her tone was soft but sounded oddly sad.

Again I looked over to B, to catch her brown-black eyes. But she was looking straight ahead. And then I realized what I'd sensed, but had not yet put my finger on. She had an almost frowning look, yet there was something serene in this expression, this look which surfaced after she'd said something so cheerily, laughing the young teenager she was. It was a dark, hesitant element. A wistful defeated look which affected me like some wound from my own past. Or did I imagine?

Steve was kind, generous in a matter-of-fact way with his silence. He was not going with us, had other things to do, and 'not much interested,' but he loaded the boat at Tyee, and would pick us up later. Twenty minutes from Rupert, and B and I were watching Steve's white Dodge make a U-turn and head back to town.

'Good meeting ya, Kevin. I'll see ya later,' were Steve's parting words. He then lumbered over to his car, and turned. 'Maybe bring him down to Caper's for a beer if he's got time.'

'That's a good idea,' said B. It was that simple last touch between couples. I did not know how long they had been boyfriend and girlfriend. But they had held each other's hands as soon as they had come out of the car, and she had lightly stroked his right arm. Below me, the Skeena was much wider than I'd expected, and B and Steve lightly kissed. My evening was perfect. Could I somehow hold onto every minute here, now? I turned to look at the Skeena.

'There it is, Kevin,' B said. Straight out from the lookout we were standing on, a height of land which descended to the tall overgrowth of the riverbank, she pointed out what had brought us here together. There were two islands to the left, the larger one she called Raspberry Island. To the right the land seemed to flatten. I could barely make anything out. In the distance were dark shapes gone snowy beneath the low misty blanket of clouds.

Behind the distant shore a ridge of tall mountains rose into the clouds, the peaks obscured. A quarter of the slopes remained covered with snow. To the left the mountains towered over a wide channel. 'That's the Ecstall River,' B explained.

The river in front of us was muddy and it was surprisingly still at high tide. I had been told its swirling eddies could easily toss a fishing boat, and that the sandbars on the approach into Essington were dangerous even when Essington was large and near in view.

But from here, Essington was virtually unseeable, my family's past at last within my reach, but still out there and beyond.

B seemed instinctively to know how I was responding. 'I guess it's a way lot further out from here than you thought, huh, when, you know, when you were talking about it at the library?'

I agreed, nodding slowly, my eyes still fixed across the river.

We were silent for a half-minute or so.

'Yeah,' she eventually breathed out.

She started to make her way through the tall grass and berry bushes to the boat and looked back to me. 'So, we'll get going now. It's the right time for it.'

When she said this, I agreed, partly thinking of the tides and all. Yet I was then, in thinking, briefly puzzled, let it go.

'Okay, we better, eh?'

'You okay with this? I mean going across and all?'

'I thought Steve was going too?' The river was much larger than I'd expected. Steve's boat was large, but still a skiff and open.

'We don't have to, you know.'

'No, no. I was looking... the boat — I certainly couldn't handle it.'

'I'm from the Skeena, eh?' B grinned. 'We used to spend summer months far down the Skeena. We had a cabin back in the woods. We'd move our stuff by boat, sometimes make some deliveries. My brother and I, Dad taught us how to drive the outboard when I was still pretty young.' Her grin this time was even more gentle.

There was a faint brightness in the sky as we first set out. The boat glided smoothly with its power, but then pounded up and down against the current. Out on the water I felt absorbed, sucked in by the landscape, as if I had returned to a past I'd forgotten. And then, as suddenly, the river changed once more and it was stunningly calm. B's voice startled me.

'Those up ahead, Kevin. That one's Raspberry Island, remember?' And then she was silent. Her eyes thinned almost sleepingly closed against the wind, which had shifted with an overhanging cloudiness, a fine rainy mist. Her lips slowly pulled to a smile, opened suddenly.

'Essington,' she breathed. 'There.'

I felt the cool much more. The front of my poplin trousers, my thighs were very damp. The river seemed unmoving, though barely freckled, veiling rain to its surface.

For some reason talk had been nearly non-existent in the skiff. I had been so stunned on that journey across the river. There had been a kind of trepidation, anxiety, in my body, my lungs, and now sitting in the skiff I became more conscious of the cold clamminess in my hands, the depths of the water and the commanding enormity of the slopes. There were times I felt the words, a question, rising in me. B had been surprisingly outward with her quick sprite chatter, a clipped way of talking. I watched her, now speechless. And at this, she did not intrude upon my quiet, she demanded nothing, her presence was all.

My breaths had shortened, then at once, involuntarily my breath was held, caught with the sight of haunting forms breaking through the mist.

'Okay, almost there,' B said, as I remained transfixed by these skeletal posts, wooden pilings emerging from the water's surface.

Pale or blackened, bones, perches for seagulls, old-cut tree trunks marking a pattern to the approach. And after these words, 'Okay, almost there,' she geared down, I could feel the boat slowing beneath us. There was smell, hard to say what, for it was not a thing pronounced. Just this awareness of one's senses. And through my jaws ran cold, clear like river water, the wet of the rain as I pressed a hand to my right cheek.

When I looked over to B, she had just cut the engine, she caught my gaze. She barely opened her lips, as if to expel the smallest space of air, and it was, expressed, this kind of 'Okay?', a question filled with the reassurance and security she felt in these elements. In control, at home.

How it made so much sense to come here to walk in the past of family. Yet, as the dark pilings kept appearing almost one by one through the mist, to then surround us, my body seemed to hesitate in this skeletal landscape, as if to insist that the bones of the past are always best left alone.

As B passed by me, crouched to throw down the rope from the front, I extended my arm, tapped her on the shoulder, on her nylon jacket. It was excitement yet anxiety.

'This is good. Neat,' she said, in a bright and reassuring tone, not breaking her decided movement. 'My grandad was Maurice. Fished the halibut with Chinese and Japanese, too.'

After this, it was only a matter of a minute or so till B jumped ashore onto tide-flat mud. I followed quickly, planted my feet on the beach where my family's life had begun and then irrevocably turned with World War II, when they were uprooted, placed in the BC interior. Already I felt the sharp cold in my legs. Little remained of a town, but this was at last Port Essington.

Difficult to say, capture what ensued, in sequence and immediately afterwards. Oh, I recall first touching pilings, had to. At some point, B began collecting dead branches, dry grass, and of course I noticed, this felt... for it was as if she had this clearly in her mind, a matter of course. And though I felt this disappointment, that she would... we'd be each on our own here. The small emptiness was brief and not brute. I perhaps understood that we fill the recesses of letdown and loneliness, of small incident, we do this rather smartly.

Even then, in this slight gesture, her actions were filled with quiet, comforting. She meant we would build a fire together. She squinted her eyes into a grin. As she bent down to unload some logs and brush, she snatched another regard up at me. And a wind blowing into shore, a south wind and warmish, flicked up the hood of her nylon shell against her dark hair where it held straight up and bright blue, then fell. Behind her was smooth flat rock leading into water, and the white mist was steadily collecting, was now even obscuring the more distant pilings, ones I'd first touched. It was closing us into Port Essington, together.

We walked through the bush, ducking through the thick over-growth, grass, stinging nettle, cedar and alder. The tall berry bushes of Essington. I was excited and mesmerized by it all, and had frankly become lost. I wondered where it would lead. I could not contain the largeness of it, B's presence on this ground was in itself some-thing I was losing my own self in and then she called to me, dropping the branches, dropping them, called to me. Now it was her, her presence even in my limbs as I stood, the winds whistling through the trees.

'Kevin. Over here.'

I was watching her, fifty yards in front of me. The boardwalk was barely walkable in some places, thick with moss and rotting, impassable. Yet stretches were clean, dry and silvery white, undulating its way. The boardwalk my mother had spoken of, leading from our family's door, had also been, I learned from B, the main street, Dufferin. These were the planks I'd imagined, built above the earth and the flow of tidewater, now in front of me.

'I heard about these, B.'

We were both crouched, knees pointing up above the level of our chests. Stinging nettles were to be avoided, raspberry bushes were everywhere tangling with wire which splayed through broken slats.

And you put out your hand. I am startled by this gesture and we help each other up, leaning, stretching legs.

'Whoaaa,' we say, almost in unison.

You said: 'It's sad to see it all like this. Broken.' Later: 'That last big fire really destroyed Essington for good. That was sad because even my uncle's house was gone.'

'But for me, it's not like for you. For me, at least there's some of the planks still around.'

One piece of wood, thin, sharp, came away easily to your pull. The nail in it was bent and dark, worn but not rusted. You placed it back down, before we got up from our crouch, your hand extended to me. It startled me.

In my possession is a small charcoal-coloured stone that has been water-washed, a kind of smooth ring-shape with a perfect round hole in it, a circle, the edges also smooth without catch. B gave it to me, pressed it into my palm later, in a corner of sunlight we found in a dark abandoned building.

'Back over there — by the planks?' she answered when I asked about the stone. Her voice curled up into a question. 'Here,' she said. 'It's God's luck, uh, yeah, that too. I mean, "good" luck.' She giggled. 'My grade seven teacher in Terrace told us that. She was from England somewhere.'

'Can you imagine coming from England and ending up here?' I said. B simply shrugged.

A little further on, I said, 'My mother — she had a teacher who was from England, too. Named Miss Preston. Oh... oh my mother was born not that far from Terrace.'

'Neat.' B smiled.

And yet, at this point, my heart sank. How my mother had sometimes quietly wept in her bedroom. How I'd watched her eyes glazed with tears as she told me small stories of her life. Of her life in Skeena, as a child, then as a young woman. One summer afternoon, when I was still in primary school, I'd found her sitting on her bed, wiping her eyes.

And as we continued on, B gently leading me, I thought how I grew up watching my parents barely touch, barely speaking long together, though ours was a home forever without rancour.

'Your folks are important to you, huh Kevin? That's neat,' B said. I was taken by how sensitive and mature B seemed. And yet she was sweet, like the teenager she was.

'Sure, sure. They really are.'

We walked further, clambering, skirting a stream, exploring, probing, scavenging. I wanted traces of a past. At one point, we came to a small house, the planks, weathered, wcre solidly intact on three sides. Yet, on one side, nearly the whole wall had collapsed. Just back of here were broken fragments of Japanese crockery, thick rice bowls of white and blue. One piece, cream-coloured, delicate and fragile. I shoved a few into my pocket after wrapping them in some napkins, still smelling of Alaska black cod at the Double Happiness. B watched, smiling.

I cannot guess your feelings of that time, of how and if your mind kept advancing as mine, ahead with my body pulled along and through emotions, the mind's projection and relentless antici- pation. That moment of light. And impulse to go on. Sometimes this is good with satisfaction, but often all that stays is regret.

'There were two churches in the town back then?' you said. Your father had told you this. We were wandering around a graveyard behind what was left of one of the churches, the Meth- odist Church, a cream-coloured frame building. It would have felt so much differently, I can sense, if I'd been there alone, just the family stories of past.

You explore these things alone, your roots, family, a commun- ion — with a place — a physical thing. But the shiver of excitement is not simply that anticipation and then standing on the ground where your family's house was — or wandering along Dufferin Street, the planks fallen where once was Henry Wong's Grocery, Yamanaka's Bar, where fishermen, no matter what race, got drunk when they docked in, the shiver would come unexpected, without the thinking, you're somewhere, then a wind from behind. Quickly, the chill. The view of the facing far shore. It is what people say of ghosts of history. This is what happens when alone. I am now. I am cold.

But it was not this way, B.

Essington. Essington B. And now you have become that part, the exploration deep into the river's presence you are these thoughts, my regard, I watch you toting wood, your hair dark against the blue jacket. It is here, and feeling the presence of family in my thought: here are my family's roots, and yours. Isn't it strange, wonderful — at last I sense how kids can take up, step into the past of their parents, as if it's still alive, take over the history. That old age and dying really is... really an end to make them free — our parents — of life, with all the problems, pain.

And it is coincidence, how I've come to Rupert, to meet, then meet again, at the Double Happiness.

I ask you about yours, your family.

'The tides,' you say, 'are going to flow out soon. We gotta go with it, follow the six-hour cycle.'

We were looking out the broken window. ('I think this was the Post Office,' you said, and later, I said, 'I think you're right. There're some old stamps.' 'Neat,' you said.). You recall how your family built fires right here in this spot, you speak of sockeye and dog salmon and in your conviction there is melancholy: I can picture the colours vividly, thick dark orange roe of fat chunky salmon.

The springs of an old double bed, but no frame. We wander through another house, lives left behind. Refuse of abandoned bedrooms and parlours, from the '50s, some of it. Fragile flakes of yellowing newspapers, we discover, that come away with plaster and wallpaper, a Christmas seal stuck over a doorway. I say, 'Look, starling nests,' in the ruins, the corner of a kitchen, a dark square hole in a ceiling leading to an attic space. B and I uncovered what we could of Essington. Intimate the feel of all that, so much like companions on a holiday, faraway.

At the edge of a clearing which fanned out from the cemetery of the church, she halted. It was a broken window frame, as if from the kitchen of the house, pale blue, though the paint had flaked, was barely there. All around were broken bottles and a seeming household full of Japanese china, some things virtually intact. And we left this in the bush, where hardly were there traces of a house which must have stood here. We left it to Port Essington. All that remained was the history of families who lived by the fishing here, something which lasts, but only to come back to as a memory and atmosphere, an air which can send a shiver without warning.

The cold sharp wind. The planks scattered all about, some black and burnt from the last fire, Essington's end. Part of this, my hands traced where they could, and B — I did not separate her from this, my astonishment before a power in land and water I'd never before encountered. I was filled with immediate memory and longing, and no words came. I thought of community, the twisted rusted sheet metal of roofing, thought of natural history too. I stood in the water where for generations the Nishga and Tsimshian Indians had fished in dugout canoes, dried the sockeye on wood. I stood in the past of Chinese and English, of the Norwegian and Finnish fishing families of the north coast. Above all, Japanese Canadians. My history and B's.

'Kevin,' B called. 'You're getting wet, you're standing in the stream. Boy,' she grinned.

'Kevin, the Japanese lived around here. By the water. And the cannery...'

'God, Japanese, Chinese, Finnish — there was a Finntown, Finland — and British and Indians living together, fishing...' I thought.

'My grandparents hardly ever mixed with the Japanese or

others. In those days communities kept to themselves. Indians were separate especially. And us— well I guess... though we were more Finnish, we were kind of alone.'

'And Finntown?' I asked.

'I think there were some contacts. But we were kind of... you understand, Kevin. It was hard... I think you know what I mean.'

Her grandfather had felt so badly for the Japanese when they'd been forced to leave Essington in World War II. He'd thought of childhood friends, though as adults the groups had pretty much fallen back into their ghettoes.

And I recalled: 'Weird, eh, B? My family. When they got to Toronto after the war, they ended up in an area with lots of Finns. A Finnish family lived downstairs from them. They were kind, my parents told me. That's how he got his first job. My dad.'

I was still about ten years old, two years before my father died. He seldom spoke with many words. What he said was always precise, strong, and held the depth of his quiet. But there was one day. He talked of that past Skeena, about the segregation, about how some Japanese Canadians felt about the Indians. My father told me as we sat together on the couch: 'Indian people were very kind. They were good at fishing and never complain about Japanese. We always said Indians are quiet people. Except, some people used to say, when they drink in town. Then they get bad.'

I'd asked my father: 'You had Indian friends?'

He said: 'Once... I knew a family. But they were half-breed. Some people used to say blood never mixes. Indian? When I was young. But after, I know them at the cannery, but that was all.'

And then there's anger at your own parents, but quickly passes. He then became very silent, in a way I'll always recall. You look at them, their hands, love them. And this is grief, a moment of knowing them, of not knowing as well, their lives and personal darkness.

It was then, later, after supper, he said: 'Kevin, you... always be kind to people whatever they are, what people say about them. When Mama and I get old and then will be gone, we will be so peaceful knowing you are kind and act in proper ways.'

We were seated by the fire she'd built, B and I. Shadows had begun their descent across distant mountains, the mist seemingly clung to our gestures, our hands. In half-light was the scent of alder and scrub from the hot smoke surrounding us. At times, my breath choked from me, yet I was extraordinarily tranquil. And B became very sad in the eyes: 'We had to — my family didn't live in town like the Japanese or others. They had to come from so far. My mum, she walked to the general store in town when she was young. It was so hard in the winter.' She then became silent, looked more intently to the fire.

We both sat, listened, as even the fire's crackling of pitch faded into the forest silence.

At the window, B and I were standing together, our arms by our own sides. At the window, I stared at the crack. It had been taped. Her eyes fixed to the right, she said, 'Raspberry Island.' I continued to stare in the direction of the crack. She talked about how she seldom spent long periods out in the bush now. Only rarely would she go into the backwoods. 'Up that way,' she pointed vaguely into the mountains. It was where her grandmother still lived, alone. It was how B kept alive her past, through the past of her grandmother. Her eyes remained fixed on the island in the Skeena. My eyes flicked to the same object of regard, Raspberry Island, and she was now quiet for some time and my eyes returned to the fractured glass. There was a sense of ponderous weight in my limbs, my arms. There was still enough sunlight, it was against the blue of her jacket. She appeared weightless. I'd never seen the Skeena as still.

I turned towards her, grabbed her hand, lightly pressed, feeling a delicate ring with a small stone, immediately thought of Steve. Her gaze remained in the distance.

'Thanks, for all this, B,' I said. 'You know... you're nice,' was all I managed to clumsily utter.

I kissed her lightly on her forehead, then softly touched her temples, gently pushing back her hair. My hands gripped loosely around her two arms, but my muscles felt insistent.

'Steve?' she said with question.

When people asked, back out east, my family asked me, I said: 'Yeah, I want to go again.' I told them I had been overwhelmed by Port Essington. It was the truth.

I told them about the kindness of my young friends, '"B," funny name, eh?' I said. 'And her boyfriend, Steve.'

What I told seemed worth telling. Those simple things possible to faithfully communicate.

Now as I lie here on my back I am filled with missing and sadness. I do want to go back. It was my family's home. And now something of me is there. Among the broken things of lives, community. The berry bushes. The muddy flats, the pilings, the crockery fragments.

She was just a young girl who came briefly into my exploration which had begun years ago. But it ended up as so much more. The day I left Rupert, caught the ferry for the Digby Island airport, I saw a young family, parents, their kids — a girl of likely twelve, loading furniture onto their boat docked at the floats by the Fishermen's Co-op. I imagined her family, the crusty orange roe from dog salmon.

She was just a teenager I met once. But...

'This is really important to me, you know, Kevin?'

I nodded.

'I wish Steve'd come.'

'Uh-huh,' I grabbed her left arm lightly. I said, 'I like him — he seems really great, B.'

She shot her eyes to the side, bit her bottom lip with her small delicate teeth. 'He's going, he's saving money, 'cause he might be going to the college? You know, in town. I mean Terrace,' said B.

We were walking once more, those remnants of the silvery wooden boardwalk which pushed into the bush. I thought of those words of my father, heard again the crackling of pitch pine of the fire B had built. The sound of pitch pine, the wistful voice of my mother is what fills my heart at this instant.

Why is it that these things never seem to leave you? I stare up at the ring of movement, the bracelet, the glittering yellow of a Paris morning, where only now it has again come to mind, the dust... how it presses upon my heaving chest.

The moments, the few seconds of awakening, hold an extraordinary intensity. Sight, smell, taste take profound possession, penetrate, jar. Hearing. An alarm, a radio, babies crying, those things which wake us whether by choice or not. And it is, however, the breathing, the feeling in the chest that seems to be part of the awareness of consciousness, the sense of brought to, alive, and this extreme intensity then spans the body, to trigger the senses resolute. The eyes blink open, ears begin to thrum, as sounds become decipherable and start the body into its more waking rhythms. Your arm is outstretched, the hand tightly clenched, holding.

I lie here on my back in this dusty Paris room and the muddy Skeena still drifts in my body, though it was some years ago now.

I close my eyes tight, light refracts through the window above the rue Geoffroy. The recollection of the Essington night remains incomplete. And I dream with such untelling, the empty places within the narrative repeat still stubborn, relentless, occupied.

It was very late before B had decided the tides were right for the crossing back to Tyee.

'I gotta be careful, eh, Kevin? All kindsa bad sandbars around here. Winds can get pretty rough in some parts, out in the open. But water's deep now. We oughtta go out, eh, with the tide. Top of the cycle.'

The sun had been out at well past ten in the evening, but now the darkness came suddenly over the Skeena River. From rocks near an old rusted oil tank, we gazed down at deep water. It chopped at the shore, driven by the force of west winds. I was scared in the skiff as we set out, the violent rocking back and forth, but I tried to hide this with a grin. My head was numb.

'It's been great, eh, B?' I said. The up and down pounding of the skiff threw water onto me, though I sat crouched beneath the windshield. If B recognized my expression, she said nothing.

Some minutes later though, the Skeena suddenly became miraculously calm. A half-moon shone fiercely, entrancing light, towards the wider waters downriver opening to Cassiar, the Gitsen Cannery, then Port Edward and Prince Rupert. It's said when the moon is full or new, there's a big tide on the Skeena. Here it was only a half, but already it was big and generous with our need to quickly return.

I thought back to the library at Rupert. The damp trousers, buying coffee at the all-night Chevron, stretching out in the hotel, the satisfaction. 'I know what you mean, the smell of salmon, the canneries and all,' B had said, and it clanged in my chest. But then, B was beside me. She was silent, seemed without thoughts, her face radiant and at ease as she stared into the sky.

My eyes closed, I said, 'River's good to us tonight.' Immediately, the pretense, the dumbness rang loud and I opened my eyes. But B said nothing, offered only her gentle presence.

'Thanks,' I said, and then it was like those earlier moments that day in the cabin. I reached out to her.

I did not want to alarm her. That would not be good. Yet, I felt such growing necessity. My hand, out to her, stroked B's hair, fell to her shoulders, reassuring her, as her face, I think, remained expressionless, though not resistant.

'Please Kevin,' she said very quietly. She leaned back, raising her hand slightly as much warning as prohibition. A sad look came to her eyes. Her sigh was barely audible. And here I felt so sure, to take this step, a decision all my own. I asked her to cut the engine.

A soft murmur became barely audible over the river sound. As she bent down, behind her it seemed as if the sky above the nearby mountain briefly flared with a beautiful, magical light. She turned, her face in that moment, I felt, had changed, welcomed me.

We lay together on the floor of the boat, only its rocking beneath us. The moon was clear above as the skiff began to once again settle under us to the Skeena's pattern. I knew what I wanted, to stay like this through the night. I believed, felt in my body, the natural, the laws, so to speak, which had controlled our meeting from two evenings before. We drifted towards the Tyee shore. Then, I drew B firmly against me.

The recollection of the Essington night remains incomplete. But even now, as it was then, my body feels the odd enchanting cool of B's skin, my fingers wandering over her, falling asleep this way, dreaming that I would wake into the morning on the Skeena, River of Mists, B in my arms.

And it is, however, the breathing, the feel in the chest that seems to be part of the awareness of consciousness, that you are brought to, alive, and this extreme intensity then seems to span the body, and the senses resolute, sight — the eyes which blink open — the hearing — as sounds become decipherable and trigger the body into its more waking rhythms. This awareness of the body, an arm stretched out, hand tightly clenched, holding.

First the cold. My own fingers feel it, chill, though out of sleep my body seemed wrapped in a reassuring soft warmth. I awoke without memory of dream, there was sadness. Yet, as I slowly became more conscious, the deep satisfaction of the night before brought me back.

'Kevin. Kevin, we'll sleep like this together, we'll dream. Forever.' These words, words still there, as if clinging to the lungs.

I kept my eyes shut, intent, wanted to, this warmth, a humidity over my skin, though there seemed both a cold at my thighs, perhaps an odd burning, itch too on my penis. I called out, not loudly, 'B,' and heard only the forests swaying. Three times without reply. Slow rhythms of trees, twigs, it was a silence which engulfed my heart immediately with the deep penetration of dread.

I called out a final time.

At once I became aware of the cold in my outstretched right hand, aware of a dry thing. And yet my abdomen and lower legs remained warm, humid. Without opening my eyes, yet without retracting my outstretched limb, my own voice heaved. Involuntarily it churned from my bowels. I retched. A sharp pain caught at my right shoulder, an instant, an acute cramp, the kind that freezes one momentarily, feels even intestinal, yet it will pass, relax, smooth out. We only wait. But I did not wait. My bowels again. Even upon the breath, my first wail, propelled by all my strength. Yet so feeble, barely a sound. And in that instant one thing became clear. B was not there. She had gone.

I opened my eyes to the touch of my hand. I thought of rock. Then perhaps it was of branch, tree. But then, my right hand began to violently shake. There in my right hand, resting beneath my thumb and finger, where I'd remembered her palm, her gentle tug, was cold rigidity. I knew it suddenly. It was bone. The bone of a human skull.

How had the warmth I had woken to been drained from me? In my wrist was dry ice which shot its searing to thumb and fingers.

But now I did not cry out. Did not cry out more, in resignation, heavy sadness, my breathing short and caught. Now my entire body was as my hand. All was still.

The bone was neither marked by flesh, nor yellowed and pocked. It was smooth, cool, possibly pleasing to the touch. And there, in my waking, I felt, saw it. The brown hair— B's. Caught in the early light, it sparkled. I was oddly tranquil.

And so suddenly there was breeze, B's hair blowing, strands began to cover my face, my opened mouth, adhered to my cheek. And I wanted to taste. I bit, I licked. Saw her face as it once was, in the car, upon the bank, in the light of an Essington ruin, in the light of a memory. I felt compelled to swallow, wanted to fill my throat, gloriously suffocate this hair, her hair. The concave forms of the skull repelled me, yet I longed to hold onto their beckoning recess. And my eyes suddenly filled with the longing, the swelling of heart, the emptiness in my bowels, the remorse...

What is it then, just a letter, 'B.' 'B.' It is carved now into the tale that is my willing, my desire for another's touch into my heart, so thick in the lungs.

'Just "B," the letter?'

'Yup, just the letter. I should explain, Kevin.' And then, 'You, you talked about the smell of salmon and the canneries?' I could hear the upward lilt of the questioning. 'B,' you spoke of your dad, a fisherman like mine, the coincidences of life which you said made us connected by the river, always, because of history, what 'they' had done. And you said, 'Let's go to Essington, whatcha think?'

What is it in this dust, caught in my throat and lungs, how you, I, things stay, stay, circling, in the air, the hot humid summer disease. My Paris.

It was already mid-morning in Prince Rupert, the busiest sections of 3rd Avenue and 2nd. I walked past the Woolworth's, the Greek restaurants, the young Rupert fishermen and women in town for a few days, headed for breakfast at the twenty-four-hour Moby Dick Coffee Shop. Shoppers beginning to drift into Rupert Square Mall. I looked without aim at clothes — blue jeans — at pots and pans, drank refills of coffee. I wanted the busyness of day and people,

people, yet had no will to talk to a soul, speak of where I had been, had visited.

Hours earlier, a passing truck had stopped for me on Highway 16 at Tyee. I ran thankful to those blinking tail-lights, felt the rush of telling in my chest. I climbed in the cab and then at once came falsely cheery with few words. The driver, an Indian from Williams Lake, carting frozen poultry, asked about my abandonment there on the road, and when I fell silent he turned, I thought, cold, probably even to the touch, but I could not do other and we both looked straight ahead, he turned up the radio, drove the remaining ten kilometres without words.

But how can one speak of things when everywhere the town goes on in its normal quotidian affairs? People queueing at the bank to pay hydro bills, a saleswoman, cellular phone and all, returning calls left overnight on her message taker. And when I'd jumped out of the cab, the driver from Williams Lake put out his hand, said, 'Hey, man, you're freezing, better get yourself a cuppa coffee. You have a good day, eh, take care,' and I swear it was pure.

At the Double Happiness — I needed to return, ask questions. About B. It was nearing 11 a.m., it was mildly hectic with coffee break, a fragment of pass-the-time chatter from a young lean woman from Stone's Menswear, and there was a young girl serving. Her hair was very black, permed into tight curls. It was the first time I'd seen her.

'Oh, I thought you see before,' the owner answered. 'She been working oh, for me oh, maybe now two years. Two summers.' He paused. 'I think you tell me you see my girl?'

'I did. Yeah, yeah,' I said. 'Yesterday, in the morning. Her name is "B." "B,"' I repeated, paused. Looked at him expectantly.

But there was no explanation.

'Hmm. No. Mistake, you.' He then just laughed, walked away. I still see the look of brief confusion on his face.

I say now that I feel the urge to go to Rupert, that I'm pulled there by roots, the history of my family's life there. But that day I wandered back into Prince Rupert, with the visit of Essington now heavy in my limbs, wanted badly to leave, to ignore any questions and thoughts which called at that terror, which sat thick at my temples beneath my eyes, ready. I was unwilling to probe further Skeena's history, but this final day in Rupert I returned to the library. It was where I'd met her, one wet Kaien Island night.

The librarian had little to show me of Port Essington papers. And it was by accident that I opened the pages of the Victoria Times-Colonist. The date, August 7, 1937. It was on page five.

A young girl had gone missing from Port Essington. She was fifteen, it said. It had occurred several months prior to this article. She had not yet been found. Someone had been questioned about the disappearance, for she had last been seen with him. The man was a Japanese fisherman named Yoshida. Masami Yoshida. My father.

Then, an Indian teenager, a Nishga from the Naas River, had been detained a short time later, then released, too. He had claimed to be the girl's boyfriend. The girl had been unnamed, but the young man, the subject of the article I was reading, had been found dead. His body had washed up on shore near Tyee. The police had called it a suicide. His name, Steven.

The girl was described as part Finnish.

'The disappearance,' I read. 'Still missing.' Into my eyes, the look in the eyes of my father, looks we seldom truly exchanged. The look I now held onto, a few days before he died in the autumn. The sun coming through the windows.

My hands touched cedar, they touched leather, they touched mud river. My hands touch all these things now, as I lower them to my abdomen, spread them to my side, hips, come to rest at my groin, along the muscle and bone there. How it is humid, thick with summer, memory and history.

And yet each day there is a kind of pull, a compulsion. I rise from my bed and minutes later descend the winding stairs from the room that I will always remember Marie-Pierre by. I do this daily, this walk, through the Left Bank and to the Seine.

My favorite café in this part of town is called Les Canons des Gobelins, at the boulevards Arago and St. Marcel. It is not so far from the Quai de la Tournelle, and near to the Moslem mosque. I position myself on a terrasse table on the side of the boulevard St. Marcel.

My life, since those days in Rupert, has been single-driven with appetite. The harsh tastes of hidden rooms at the ends of dark passageways. Up past Les Halles to St. Denis and Strasbourg, that activity in doorways and recesses of shops shut for the evening, I pass them, the prostitutes of the city. The weighty smells of frites and merguez fill the air. And then she, yes, always this she, has pushed me off, 'No, not there.' And then, 'We make love now,' she says this impatiently. 'You have to be quick, m'sieur, what do you want for 100 francs?' And when I ask her her name, only as we dress, she answers, 'Hanan,' and then I tell her mine.

And always to press my face closer, holding the thighs by both hands in an exact position and gesture, insistent, though I obey with each resistant order. ('Hanan, Hanan,' though each week, someone other.) And how I remember even now the burning in my penis as I moved into her, stretching my hands to the bedframe, that delight of a quantifiable degree of passion with such hurt, measured by fingernails, the pull red of foreskin as the towel creased beneath her, dampened beneath our weight, under a lamp clamped to the bedpost. A smell of antiseptic hung in the air.

And I arched my arm around her left leg, extending, felt the sheen yet arresting rough of the marred black nylon against my lips and dry hands, the pearl light which held to the bone of her leg.

Just a letter. B. Carved now into my tale, my will, my desire for another's touch, thick in the lungs.

'B.'

And the doctor at the clinic hands me reports of the tests, it is not serious, just the most common, but without question, disease. Yet is it not to this kind of activity that I am now compelled, unsated at end, numbed of thought and feeling, so too to lick. The sweat — the hair. In such manner have I lived this city, Paris. City of Dreams, they say. I say a place of obsessive physical need that I might, careless, burn the interminable longing of the heart.

And I can smell it and taste it still, the hair. And I taste too the thin strap of an undergarment, the thin stream of bitter fluid, the tongue pressed against, even inside her, my mouth turned more forceful, the need to clench with my teeth. I smell it as such the dull fever, wherever it lodges in the body, is still the burning, the sallying dolor of prostate, the grease and beer of night's air. In the dark yet tidy room where she, Hanan, perhaps another, has led me, signalled by a cheap rose bouquet poster, she would squeeze my testicles, fingers would trace automatically the skin of scrotum, a single finger which could be wet with dry powder or gel, her bracelet, entangled in my hairs.

When she enters, I try not to be so curious. Or at least try not to so obviously stare. Yet I crave her notice. Of course, as with many American men, it is fantasy.

She is like the young French woman I so want to meet. Most days she wears the beige poplin raincoat, a thin cotton or silk scarf, pale yellow, tossed carelessly but stylishly around her neck, and draping to her shoulders. She would likely puff hard at a cigarette, but I have never seen her smoke. How, when the heart drops to the stomach with even the inadvertent sideways glance of a woman, control falls away.

But with such excess have I become obsessed. Do I seek a way to leave behind, forget?

And yet my actions, my sole action, so feeble. A week ago I uttered my first words, something about the café always being so full, the need for more waiters, something, to her.

'Not always full, but yes sometimes, just dreadful,' she said, her smile at first seemed quick almost, sharp and patronizing, I was caught, but then it softened. I glanced at her scarf, her shoulder, and away, I felt ready to speak again, but my mouth numbed. In any case, she looked away. That was the end.

I regard her eyes most. She is like the Parsiens one often sees. French, but also something else. She is very likely part Algerian or possibly Lebanese, maybe Italian. There are, perhaps, some Oriental features. She is always a foreigner in the eyes of the French. And as I regard her, I am pulled by something else and admit my single-minded attraction. It is true: something, something.

And now I look at her, this Parisienne who tosses back her scarf, then rises to leave without even a glance of farewell. This woman, these women who remain as gestures, the clothes, the turning ankle, too visible and relentless. These women who always leave my gaze.

Prince Rupert. What cannot be left behind, what is given to me. The young man's voice, his welcome to me in the Rupert library. To be bestowed the chance to be close to family, parents, the chance to feel that inextricable link of roots, the power and domain of nature alone — the spirits of land, a river. The most tender feelings I held for 'B.' My eyes found B there in the Double Happiness, she sat, we made our plans, the most enchanted moments of my life. These words over and over in my journal, my notes. There is no forgetting. Each day, each evening.

From the door of the café it's about ten minutes to the Seine, and this, Paris by dusk, the postcard of it. I take the concrete steps which lead to the riverbank with its dark corners and alcoves of embracing couples. There is, not far from the bateaux mouches near Les Invalides, the area known as point of encounter for the homosexuals of the city. Women feel safe walking this route, Marie-Pierre once told me.

Paris, always so enticing in early evening. The bright cafés, the art-nouveau fixtures of those newly renovated, the constant excitement of too-ready tourists — Italian, Chinese, Swedish. Faux marble tabletops are littered with lager glasses or long drinks, while below, the monstrous searchlights of the bateaux mouches shine their first passes of the banks, the apartments which back onto the Seine. Crowds gather about the crêpes stands, their displayed tins of Orangina, Coca Cola and tart lemon Gini.

Still, how more enchanting the quiet, the beckoning recesses of Paris into such shadows.

So, this evening, I have, as is habit, advanced east towards Gare de Lyon, ignoring Notre Dame, the harsh gaiety of the Fifth Quarter.

True, I have taken this path so often, but today the feeling is most extraordinary. Wrapped and pulled as if by some jute cord, my heart is excited, fearful, dry. And there I have passed the last of the romantic alcoves, have not taken notice of their lovers or clochards, and suddenly I am engulfed by the utter darkness. Overhead, from a bridge, a police siren trumpets its velocity above, dying into the distant disturbance. My heart stops. I am not alone.

From this spot, fifty paces ahead of me, I am led, and without hesitation follow. I advance like some automaton, without ability to halt.

Ahead, who has led me here, she who has at last guided me from my position at the café. It is time. I must finally act. It is marvellous to follow her. Be strong. My hands, stiff at my sides, tremble with their final waiting, preparation.

In this dark silence I knock at the door. She is there.

So this. What I have seen from my bed, above my bed, before my opened eyes. Now as I walk, steadily behind her, my eyes remain still, fixed: there is the bracelet moving in a slow circle, its colours — blue, red, the movement of dust and thread glowing in the Paris sky.

I know her slim back, will know it forever and upon her shoulders, draped as scarf, in that manner French women miraculously and effortlessly do, she wears a deep magenta shawl of beautiful woven designs. So, I continue, I advance. And above and about her head I see it. This umbilical, muscular pull, the dance of the bracelet, the movement of dust and thread floating along the river.

I have been waiting, it feels, for years. I have descended from my bed, have been walking the Paris streets. It is, I know at one point, a slight and convenient curve in the river. We will come face to face. And here in her serene pleasure, she will turn to invite me further into dark, the recess.

How deep the white and suffocating cool mist which seems to fall upon just this spot on the river. How good that I will finally accept my own history, the path I have chosen to follow. And now, it is no longer my life to decide. I begin to comprehend in this strangely hot humid Paris summer, this summer of my dull malady in the chest.

When she does turn to my regard, my breath suddenly runs startlingly clear. For there is not the lovely face of a young woman. Behind this robe she is totally faceless, without eyes, nose, mouth. A head with no features of any sort; yet how full, and a suggestion of smile, of ultimate contentment. It is delicate as china, the enrapturing colour of sweet cream. And then she turns again around, continues on.

My advance is now quick. Frenzied, I race, propelled by will though in my breast my heart has fallen silent. I will finally hold her arms in my hands again, squeeze with clenched fists of a morning long ago. I close my eyes, knowing what I will see, feel the chill breeze of a mist over the river bank. I will wake again in Essington, caress that skin, the boat rocking under us.

'Wait. No, not there,' she will instruct. And I, with my own hands chapped and sore, palms dried with blood, will at last kiss this thing on the lips, the bone lips of B's skull.

And now a voice comes, out of the concave stillness, one echoing from my own empty dark, years ago, 'Masami,' she whispers, 'Masami.' And so feeble, I hear only the sad voice of my mother.

'Masami,' I repeat. And then walk on as a smile comes to my face. For my still heart is now bloodless, I am my father's name.

Gloss (B)

1

One evening, my friend Sharon and I are walking along the street, it's de Maisonneuve. It's Sunday and we're out looking for a meal, our first since her arrival from Saskatoon where her husband had effectively taken months from her life, from her own possession. One day, he had arrived home, said, 'Goodbye, dear, I'm off with a woman I'm in love with,' and suddenly, so suddenly, she was alone in her Saskatoon home by the river, standing in her shoes by the phone by the picture window, prisoner to the machine he had set in motion, the months of divorce matters, months thus absconded from my friend, and of course, more.

Sausages, frites, sauerkraut, when I suggest it, a last-minute flash of an idea, is all she wants to fill the emptiness of a particularly bleak day. 'Just what I need,' she tells me with a smile which she muscles to support. And beneath our tongues we both seem to know of the lack of the forcefully peppery and tart which can jump-start our lives when we linger too long on the dull confections of loss.

We pass darkened discos, not yet open, Pacha Club, I notice, lit up restaurants, open for business but empty, and the cars are coming past us, one way.

And it's on this route that she says to me, with a voice which has clearly forgotten briefly her private dismay, 'Did you see her, her eye, that woman we just passed?'

'Huh?' I cleverly respond.

'The woman who just passed us. She didn't have her left eye and I think it was just black, empty. Oh, God, usually you don't see that, people have it covered up with dark glasses,' she says.

I am not sure whether I noticed, and it's rather unlikely I did. I tell her I wasn't really looking carefully to notice, but maybe, hmm, I guess so, and I'm still guiding us to Chez Better, the sausages, their own natural ingredients only, micro-brewery beer.

The meal, Sharon tells me some days later, seemed to do the trick, helped her lift the chesty burden of a sad night in Montreal.

That night we hugged each other good night, went our separate ways, more sure than ever before of the healing properties of sausages, frites, sauerkraut and good strong mustard.

2

It was the Métro, Direction Honoré-Beaugrand. A family got on at Papineau or maybe Préfonatine Station it was. A husband and wife, two young children clutching their mother.

I noticed it rather immediately. She was quite thin, a pale though not unhealthy complexion upon quite visible cheekbones, slim nose. Her face caught my attention — not just because of her fairly plain cheery attractiveness, made more so by her sketched lips playfully smiling as she caressed her children as they shifted restlessly about on the seats. It was her eyes — for as she, at some juncture, slanted her head in my direction, it struck me that she had no left eye — or perhaps, less likely, a very black false one. My judgement was that where her left eye once had been, was darkness for others to see, a black recess which doubtless did not join the focus of her right eye's gaze.

I thought how pretty she might have been — might have — I caught myself thinking this. She seemed to draw me in with the beauty of her presence, her normalcy, which was yet marked by the doom of potential, as if what was missing added up to less.

And so, how daily women catch my attention and they are considered in such ways through a man's eyes, the account of physical appearance: the eyes, nose, bust, hips, legs, ankles. And how so much this one day, this woman here left eye vacant, is no different a brief Métro passenger, who had dressed her young children for an outing, yet more visibly and physically marked by her own darkness and ours, shining through her heart.

At Métro Station Pie IX, I descended, for I was on the route to the Botanical Gardens and it was Sunday, a week after I had met my friend Sharon, from Saskatoon, for dinner.

3

The masks I saw at the Japanese Pavillion at the Botanical Gardens of Montreal. Period. Full Stop. I so think of punctuation, that I am breathless.

The masks surprised me, for they were uh, so familiar, so much history pushing out of the sand at my feet. I was standing wet in leaky shoes; and soon they grew more familiar, such faces! All of them, in a row, for they were Japanese, they were tranquil in a row, tranquil or laughing, or sarcastic, or angry, or diffident, and they were there under glass cases aligned at a level, these masks from the Noh Theatre.

Such masks are often of pure white unblemished faces, like fragile china. There are thin eyes (So Nipponese!) and I thought how eerie, like the white make-up faces of theatre, of masque. Yet in every way each mask was like every face, of others, the ghosts of others, that in this once upon a time Sunday of a dozen or so facial expressions, their white haunting, they are us as we are at every point in life, that we are dying and ghost. And they looked me in the eye and though I nor they held mirrors to trick, these were images of what I was next to become.

Here were faces, so pale yet full, and I was abdomen and emptiness. I closed my eyes and saw where an eye once was, which therefore now does not gaze, and my heart filled with desire for that dark recess of where the tongue could reach and lick, place-holder for the vacuum that is luminous sheath, pubis no longer, the unsated itch.

4

The day before my visit to the Botanical Gardens and the perform-ance of the Noh Theatre, I think. It occurs to me where I was, it was the Japanese Canadian Buddhist Church on St. Urbain. And I'm eating Nihonshoku with my cousins who, for all these years before I'd moved to Montreal, were my connection to this place. I'm eating a bowl of noodles, I'm eating chirashi— a mazze-gohan, chicken teriyaki and some tempura. There are big pots of green tea on the tables.

'Hey, you finally made it to our bazaar,' says one of my cousins. And everywhere, they're there, they're here, cooking food, serving it, moving chairs, there are those long utilitarian folding tables in this church basement like they are in church basements everywhere.

It's here that other Niseis are introduced to me. 'He's our cousin from Toronto. His father was our father's younger brother,' they explain.

And somebody says to me, 'You were born in Toronto, eh? I didn't think you had any Port Essington in your face.

'I was born there,' he says. 'Last time I went back was before the fire. There were some Finnish people still, living in Finntown. A few Indians, too. But now I don't know.'

I watch the Noh actors moving with their highly stylized abrupt gestures, one character confronted by another, a spirit speaking in precise cadence from beneath a pure white mask. A high-pitched flute sound, the percussive deliberate smack of hand striking wood.

'There were some Finnish people still, living in Finntown. A few Indians, too. But now I don't know.'

I think, 'Essington.'

'B.'

5

Back in 1986, a few of us, writers living alone in Toronto, founded a dinner club, that is, we got together pretty regularly for dinner. It was called The Coincidence Club. It lasted for only a year or so. The founding members were:

> Mary di Michele
> Joy Kogawa
> Margaret Hollingsworth
> David McFadden (it was his idea)
> and me, Gerry Shikatani.

Mary, like me, lives here in Montreal now.

Joy, how are you? Japanese Canadian you, who spent the war years in Slocan like my family, Joy, how are you?

I used to bump into Margaret on the streets of Toronto. Margaret from England, who ended up in Nelson, BC, in the Kootenays not far from Slocan, where she met David McFadden. Margaret who, too, has been up there to Rupert, spent time in that place called Skeena...

David, how always my mind will at times recollect The Coincidence Club, you, David, how are you doing, my dear David?